A Mortally Wounded Heart

J. A. Cherbonneau

PublishAmerica
Baltimore

© 2010 by J. A. Cherbonneau.
All rights reserved. No part of this book may be reproduced, stored in a retrieval system or transmitted in any form or by any means without the prior written permission of the publishers, except by a reviewer who may quote brief passages in a review to be printed in a newspaper, magazine or journal.

First printing

All characters in this book are fictitious, and any resemblance to real persons, living or dead, is coincidental.

PublishAmerica has allowed this work to remain exactly as the author intended, verbatim, without editorial input.

Hardcover 978-1-4512-0034-8
Softcover 978-1-4512-0035-5
PUBLISHED BY PUBLISHAMERICA, LLLP
www.publishamerica.com
Baltimore

Printed in the United States of America

6/11/10

Laurie —

I hope you enjoy reading this as much as I did writing it.

You are & always be the most honest person I ever met!

J. A. Charbonneau

Dedication

For my children and grandchildren who
have made my life complete.

Prologue
"One Last Sunrise"
1970

Olivia shivered fruitlessly, in an effort to ward off the bitter, biting, ferocious blizzard-like wind that overpowered her body as she wrapped her drab, gray, pathetically threadbare coat more tightly around herself. With robotic steps, in her trance-like state, she cautiously walked in her well worn heavy winter boots along the hardened earth below. Only a few short months before, this tan colored, grainy beach had been soft and welcoming, but now, in fact, was frozen, forbidding, hard, and unyielding under her footsteps. Olivia continued her journey automatically, without delay, and approached the snow-covered boulders, her safe haven, that bordered the cold black depths of the frigid icy lake below. This had been the same beach where she basked in the sun and surf so many years ago, she recalled, as her pace quickened to reach her destination before first light.

Just that morning she had been at this same site, savoring the brilliant splendor and excitement of another colorful sunrise, the one last sunrise she would ever see.

Olivia was harshly brought back to the present time. The beauty of the morning's splendor forgotten for the moment. Numbness overwhelmed her whole body, heart, and soul; the blizzard-like conditions worsening by the moment. Snow and fierce winds swirled around her, a winter-wonderland of Christmas-like fairies dancing and flying through the pitch, total darkness of the midnight sky. The brutally harsh wind attempted to force her backward, away from the lake, so it seemed. Olivia struggled to continue forward against the blast of glacial Arctic air and raised her frostbitten face to savor the wintry, merciless, savage, biting air as it seemingly played with her long, auburn hair that swirled and caressed her face. She approached the enormous granite stone to sit and reflect upon the final day, the one last sunrise she had seen. Another, she would never see.

The explosive sunrise that morning had been exquisite, she fondly remembered, tightening the grip on her thin winter coat at the same time burying her hands in her pockets. Without hesitation, she also dipped her feet into the soothing, but crisp, icy water before her without seeming to notice or care.

The wispy, fleeting clouds she witnessed at daybreak had been highlighted with crimson red, sapphire blue, and silver gray, as the sun caressed the mountaintop and exploded over the ridge and blanketed the snow covered ground, reflecting, illuminating, its brilliance against the icy covered branches of the trees over the valley below. The tree limbs appeared to have been blessed with sparkling diamonds, she remembered from her morning adventure to this site.

Sitting on a snow covered rock, the midnight-ink, the depths and emptiness of the gloomy water before her now became one with the velvety moonlit sky that was dotted with tiny, twinkling, playful planets.

Olivia was mesmerized by the stars and the brilliant full moon that filtered through the windblown snow and blizzard conditions. Those heavenly bodies where presently her only companions and had been her only friends since she could remember. Now, she and her friends would be united in peaceful splendor. She smiled, but with tears cascading down her frozen cheeks as she raised her arms, painfully, with gracelessness toward her friends in the sky. The sub-zero temperatures had stiffened her body, but none the less, her nearly frozen fingers reached out to touch the full moon in the heavens that continued to beckon her.

With frigid finger tips, she felt the softness of the sky that reminded her of that black velvet dress she had once had, as a child. Her last party dress…her one and only fancy dress. Never a formal prom dress or satin wedding dress had she owned. There had never been a need for any other dress but that one lonesome velvet dress with the petticoats underneath she wore for her sixth birthday party.

The brutal, icy, wind subsided for a moment and Olivia heard a mournful dog howl and a muffled, lonesome, haunting train whistle sound off in the distance. At the same moment, Olivia clearly heard melodic bells ringing from the small, brown-stone church, where she had been baptized, so long ago. As mysteriously as everything else she had witnessed in the past few moments, a choir of angels suddenly appeared before her and she sang the beautiful verses of Ava Maria with them while tears cascaded down her frostbitten cheeks.

Those were the only sounds, other than the forceful, pounding waves, from the lake, that consumed more of her frost bitten feet and at the same time she stood up and let the waves crash against her legs and thighs. Slowly, the frigid body of water consumed more of her body while she continued to gaze, with wide-eyed wonder, at her friends that winked at her from the sky, light-years… an eternity from here.

She knew she would never see another wondrous, phenomenal sunrise or see the snow gently fall to the ground as it was now, blanketing the harsh, unforgiving terrain nearby.

Olivia knew she would never lay in the snow and fan her arms and legs to make a snow angel ever again. She would never catch the softly, drifting snowflakes from Heaven with her tongue, those that did not melt on her uplifted face, first.

She realized she would never hear the sleet and frozen rain pelt the roof top and cover the ground, to make for perfect sledding or see a pond frozen, adored with skaters all dressed in their warmest clothes, glide over the glassy surface with elegance, grace, and style.

Olivia would never savor the taste of piping hot chocolate with miniature marshmallows floating on top, hear her favorite Christmas carols sung by choirs of angelic voices, or eat Ginger Snaps followed with a snowball chaser, or hang her lonesome Christmas stocking on the mantle of a fireplace, ever again.

Olivia waded farther out in the depths of the pitch black water; the waves caressed her body, welcoming her, encouraging her deeper…deeper still.

With her eyes glued to the bright, full moon and flitting from one star and galaxy to another, Olivia knew she would never see the majestic autumn leaves; the collage of fire engine reds, yellow golds, emerald greens, or spicy, brunt oranges on a mountainside or embrace this lake, again. Olivia would never be a witness to the miracle of a prism of color, exploding in the sky in the late afternoon…never another rainbow to cherish.

A summer picnic in an isolated, open field, a lazy day on this beach, or painful, blistering sunburn soothed with fragrant coca butter and baby oil…those days were long gone, now.

To see and caress the face of her newborn baby, a colt in the field, or herd of lambs grazing on a hillside…gone, too.

A tender, alluring smile; warm, masculine arms holding her tight; tender, demanding lips, united with desire pressed against her own; flesh on flesh as one, wrapped in the depths of passion, want, need, and lust…gone…gone…gone.

As her heart had once been submerged with ultimate affection and exploding with love by the man she worshiped, Bobby Dragon, the water now caressed her entire body as she floated toward the bottom of the lake she had loved so much. Floating, drifting away from a heart filled with overwhelming sorrow and pain; an emptiness to match her body. Her heart had long ago left her body. A shell had existed for more years than she had known; void of any feelings one way or another. Joy, happiness, fear, sadness…they were all one…they were all nothing.

Even through the blackness of the bottomless pit of doom, she sank to the depths below, the water gently rocked and cradled her as a mother with a babe in her arms. At the same time, the stars and the brilliant full moon where still visible to her as she slid deeper and deeper in the satiny, ebon, darkness below. Eerily silent, the water continued to caress…to cradle Olivia…her entire being.

Her loving friends were there…they had always been there…they had been the only ones…always there, waiting for her to come home.

The sun was peaking, rising over the snow covered mountain top, now and a new day was on the horizon. The amber globe of light illuminated to the bottom of the black pool that was surrounded by boulders and snow covered trees. The sun rose from the east one last time at the same time the light radiated over Olivia's being…a hint of a smile on her blue, lifeless lips…a twinkle in her glazed, emerald green eyes.

Olivia was with her loving, true friends, now. The warm sun, mysterious moon, and the twinkling stars. Those heavenly bodies were her friends…her family.

Her smile glowed from the sun that now warmed the earth so far below. Olivia had finally found peace, love, and happiness. She was home…she was the one last sunrise!

Bobby
2003

Olivia was back to haunt him. He could feel her presence, smell her seductive perfume inside the stifling cab of his magnificent Peterbuilt tractor that was attached to the fully loaded trailer. A trailer, he owned and was privately contracted by the United States government to make timely deliveries from the harbor in Boston, Massachusetts to one specific destination in California.

Panic seized his entire being while droplets of perspiration gathered at the folds of his weary, but beautiful soft blue eyes. Eyes that had been the magnet for many women in his life, but only one woman had he returned feelings of limitless love and passion. Sadly, this same woman left without saying goodbye or giving any reason why. She might as well have stabbed him in his heart or slit his throat, he told himself, time and time again because he died the day his sweet, gentle, Olivia ended her own life.

Tears filled his eyes, rolling down his cheeks and the sun-darkened interstate, the melted ribbon of highway before him, became obscure from his vision. Automatically, he down-shifted and applied the Jake brake to gain control of the best and only friend he had, his Peterbuilt tractor, to prevent it from careening off the highway into the parched, dry earth of the surrounding desert floor. All eighteen wheels of this beautiful, graphically expressive designed tractor-trailer unit dug into the bubbling asphalt below…smoke pouring from each brake pad while the 600 horsepower engine slowed to a sudden halt.

The majestic artwork on the entire trailer, a metal canvas of sorts, depicted the Vietnam Wall with various American monuments in the distant background. Nothing on this expressive masterpiece overshadowed the Vietnam Wall…nothing, and that had been Bobby's intention when he designed the project from scratch, many years ago.

Without hesitation, Bobby jumped from the cab into the middle of the deserted highway as if the seat of his pants were on fire while he tore his tight black, perspiration soaked, tee shirt, that molded itself to his muscular, fifty two year old body, off his chest before dropping to his knees to the pavement below.

This six foot former Marine sniper bent over and with every ounce of strength he had, tried to catch his breath. Post Traumatic Stress Syndrome, they called it, but Bobby knew these panic attacks he had, had nothing to do with his years as one of the most decorated Marine snipers the Corps had ever produced. It had nothing to do with his achieving the fame of being one of the most famous marksmen the world had ever known. It had nothing to do with over seventy confirmed kills he never discussed. It had nothing to do with the two purple hearts he received, nearly losing his life on both occasions.

These assaults on his body and mind had nothing to do with achieving the rank of Master Gunnery Sergeant during his twenty year military career that ended the same day he bought his first tractor trailer rig and left for parts unknown, nearly fourteen years ago. He had taken refuge in the military for eighteen years prior to his retirement to avoid going back to his hometown. There was no reason to go back after Olivia… His escape route had been the open highway and would be, he realized, until the day he died.

The panic attacks had nothing to do with not having the stability of a place to call home or even going back to his hometown the day after the funeral of the woman he loved. It did have everything to do with that same woman, though, the one and only woman he ever loved, Olivia, who went to live among the stars and the moon, thirty two years ago in the month of December.

Darkness caressed the distant Arizona mountain tops while Bobby gathered his wits and enough strength to struggle inside the cab, re-start the engine and pull the massive beast off the road for the night. He knew this was going to be one of those nights...another night of frightful dreams, tears and pain in his heart and soul.

The aging, but muscular man broke the seal of a bottle of whiskey and poured himself a glass...he always used a glass...and swallowed the entire amount in one gulp. The heat from the liquor eased the pain in his heart and after four glassfuls, the pain in his head began to lessen.

Bobby rummaged around in the sleeper section of his tractor and found his AK-47, slammed a fully loaded magazine, into it and once again left the confides of the cab as a lonesome tractor trailer drove past. This was the only vehicle to speed down the highway, this late at night, in the past two hours. Bobby raised the assault weapon in an honorary salute as the eighteen wheeler blared its air-horn in a cheerful, but startling salutation as it continued on its journey in a westerly direction.

The former Marine sniper gathered up the now empty bottle of whiskey, several empty cans he had saved from previous meals and marched into the cooling desert sands and placed the various potential sniper targets, soon to be victims, in haphazard locations near and far.

As if marching in formation with his sniper team, the retired Master Gunnery Sergeant paraded back to the highway, stopped, facing forward, away from the soon-to-be victims and lay down in the road, behind his truck. This was the only cover he could secure, but he knew "The Wall", as he called the eighteen wheeler, had never let him down before.

For more than fifteen minutes Bobby lay in wait. He knew there were more Viet Cong out there, waiting to join the empty bottle of whiskey and old soup cans. He could wait. He waited more than ten hours at different times, just for the wind to change directions to proceed undetected in Vietnam. This was a 'piece of cake' he thought to himself. "Those bastards will come out of their hiding place, soon," he whisper to himself.

Bobby inched his way to the side of the highway, but his movements would have gone undetected by anyone standing right beside him. He crawled seemingly without going anywhere. His body was as still as stone, but he was moving toward the target zone.

His breath was so shallow, only tiny particles of sand moved as each lung-full of air was released from his nose. This mouth never moved; his ears listened for the faintest sound; his skin and strands of his jet black hair signaled the change in the wind direction and he knew it was time to attack his victims before they detected him by the fragrance of his aftershave. If he had known sniping these 'pirates of death' tonight were to be his latest assignment he would have known better than to apply his favorite cologne. He knew this was not really his favorite cologne…it had been Olivia's favorite, he recalled as another tear filled his left eye and he looked down the scope of his specially designed assault weapon and without so much as any part of his body moving he slowly and gently squeezed the trigger and fired; shattering the empty booze bottle.

"There, you fucking son of a bitch," he said out loud and continued to fire into the innocent cans without so much as taking one single breath.

Still laying prone in the desert sand, he noticed various desert creatures scampering because of the exploding metal and glass debris. Without hesitation, Bobby ended their simple existence with one bullet each. "One shot, one kill," he said out loud. The motto all Marine snipers lived by.

Bobby turned over on the desert floor and lay facing the moon and star-filled sky and cradled the weapon in his arms, as he had done with Olivia, on so many occasions during their courtship, so many long years ago. He lay there and saw her face in the full moon as racking sobs escaped from his lungs for more than an hour before he fell asleep beside the deserted desert highway.

Blinding lights shone into his tear stained eyes as he struggled to waken and comprehend where he was. He knew this was not Vietnam…it couldn't be he reasoned. There were no Highway Patrol cars in Vietnam he quickly surmised while he stared down the barrel of a saw-off shot gun that was pointed at him by a young law enforcement officer who looked more frightened than the bottle of whiskey had.

"Throw that weapon away and get up!" the carrot topped trooper demanded.

"You don't ever throw a weapon, son," Bobby said and continued to hold his specialized assault rifle in his hand and quickly got to his feet.

"I said, put that weapon down or I will shoot!" the trooper screamed with panic in his voice.

"Have you ever killed anyone, son?" Bobby asked softly and with tenderness as if he were talking to a baby.

"No, but I will if you force me to!"

"Yes, that is how I justified killing seventy some-odd victims," Bobby said and carefully began to wipe the dirt from the barrel of his weapon. "I was forced to and I don't regret it…not for one minute."

"You have killed over seventy men?" the trooper cried in hysteria.

"No, not all men…some women and children," Bobby said and defiantly sauntered toward his truck.

"What the fuck are you talking about?"

"Ever hear of Nam?" Bobby demanded and glared at the young trooper while he pointed to his Vietnam Memorial on wheels.

"Oh my God!" the trooper said. "You killed that many people over there?" he asked while walking over to the tractor trailer and admired the exquisite mural that honored those who made the ultimate sacrifice so many long years ago in a land so far from home.

"Probably more; I lost count," Bobby answered callously.

"May I ask what you are doing with that illegal weapon and why were you laying asleep beside the road?"

"This is not illegal for me. It is mine and it will be buried with me, son and I was laying asleep beside the road because I was waiting for the VC to try to attack me on my right flank and by God, you snuck up on me," he responded and began to howl with laughter. "Shit, I must be losing my grip," he added. "Who would have believed it...Master Gunnery Sergeant Robert Dragon run over by a fucking cop car in the middle of a moon lit night, in the desert. That would have been totally humiliating and my men would have been ashamed to have ever known me," Bobby said sadly.

"Are you on medication or ill?" the trooper asked sincerely.

"No, to both questions, but I am sure there are those who would disagree with those answers," he added and laughed.

"What did you say your name is?" the trooper asked with a puzzled look on his face.

"What the hell is it to you?" Bobby asked.

"I just...," the trooper began.

"Identify yourself, son!" Bobby barked.

"My name is Trooper McAllister, sir!" he said and saluted.

"What branch of the service were you in, son?" Bobby asked, knowingly.

"The Marines, sir? Is there any other?" the trooper said and smiled.

"No, son, there isn't!"

"I was with the 3rd Marines, sir!" McAllister yelled in response.

"Well, if you were with the 3rd Marines, you know who I am, then don't you?"

"Sir, yes, sir!" McAllister shouted. "You are a legend, sir."

"Legends are for heroes, son. I am neither...a legend or a hero," Bobby said and got inside his truck and started the engine.

"Master Gunnery Sergeant Robert Dragon!" McAllister whispered; hero worship in his voice, in his eyes, and in his soul. "I can't believe it!" he whispered, dumbfounded, into the wind as the tractor trailer eased from its parked position and gained momentum as it continued on its journey, westward.

Jason McAllister ended his midnight to seven shift and raced toward his home only two miles from the State Police Barracks...S-Troop, as it was known.

Jason burst in the front door, frightening his pregnant wife.

"Jason, what's wrong?" his wife, Livy, asked.

"Where's that old trunk of stuff your mother left you?" he demanded rudely.

"Excuse me, Trooper McAllister?" Livy asked when her husband was being arrogant, demanding, and police-like.

"I'm sorry, sweetheart," Jason said and hugged and kissed his wife.

"That's a little better," Livy responded even though she didn't like his attitude.

"Please help me find that trunk. I need to see some things," Jason said mysteriously.

"What in heaven's name would you need to see that old stuff for now?"

"I have to read some letters and newspaper articles that I know were in there," Jason answered.

"Jason, I threw all that stuff out when we were making the nursery over."

"What!" Jason yelled. "Oh, no!" he cried in a fit of near hysteria.

"What is…was…so important about that old trash?" Livy said angrily. She never knew her mother, but she hated her and always would. She left her as an infant to be raised by strangers. For that, she would never forgive her mother.

Not only did Livy not know her mother, she never knew who her father was, either. This saddened her more than the fact her mother had 'thrown' her away because she had no idea where to begin to look for her father. She had searched for the last twenty years for her mother, but that search had been fruitless.

"God damn it!" Jason screamed and ran out the door and sped off, without any explanation, in his patrol car into the new day's dawn.

Bobby pulled off the highway into the parking lot of a Highway Hotel as the heat of another new day began to bear down on the confines of the tractor's cab. He needed to have the air-conditioning unit serviced before long. The cooling system was not working adequately and he had suffered enough, he reasoned, as he climbed out of the cab and checked into the hotel to get a hot shower and good eight hours sleep before he fell asleep at the wheel.

Using the hotel desk phone, after registering for a simple room, he called a local heavy equipment dealership to make an appointment to have the truck serviced the next morning.

Quietly, Bobby rode in the elevator toward the appropriate floor where his room was located and observed what appeared to be newlyweds, locked in a loving embrace, totally oblivious to the 'intruder' in the elevator car with them and once again was overcome with sadness. A sadness that had not escaped him since the day of his lover's funeral.

The former Marine quietly departed the elevator car, leaving the young lovers to continue their journey in life and love, while he entered his small, dark hotel room.

Bobby threw his old seabag on the bed, stripped off his dirty clothes and stood inside the shower stall while hot water caressed his tired, scarred body. A body time had been kind too, in spite of its self imposed abuse over the years. His muscles were rock hard; his stomach flat and dark hair that was just beginning to show signs of gray at the temples.

Bobby gently patted himself dry after forcing himself from the welcoming, soothing water that eased his tired body and sat on the double bed to examine the scars that were still evident from his close encounters with death in Vietnam.

There were two scars near his heart and one in his shoulder, wounds that would have killed any 'mortal' man, the doctors had told him numerous times. Bobby did not see himself as mortal…just mortally wounded…not from Vietnam, but from the loss of the one woman he loved.

Bobby turned on the air-conditioner in his room and lay naked under the crisp, white sheets while the soothing hum of the cooling system lulled him to sleep.

Bobby tossed and turned in his sleep, all that day. Images of Vietnamese children, adults, VC, jungles, rockets, sounds of exploding grenades, rifle fire and smells of death mixed with Beddle Juice, a potent painkiller the less fortunate Vietnamese used to dull the pain of rotting teeth in their heads, that were intertwined with memories of passionate kisses, making love, and promises of love, faithfulness and 'forever' were imbedded into his nightmares as they always were and always would be.

In the deepness of his fitful sleep, Bobby recalled how he met and fell in love with Olivia Bennett, the sweet, petite, black haired beauty who swept him off his feet the first time he saw her at a high school football game.

Bobby And Olivia
1966

"Where's your rifle?" Johnny Blackburn asked as the two inseparable friends left the comfort of the 1963 bright fire engine red Chevy convertible. Bobby Dragon recently purchased this oversized living room, as Johnny relentlessly teased his friend, with the hard earned money he saved by working as a 'grease monkey' at a local tractor trailer dealership.

"I cleaned it and put it in the trunk," Bobby answered. "I don't think Principal Blankenship would appreciate me strolling onto the football field with that under my arm, do you?"

"He might appreciate you a bit more, if you did," Johnny said as he threw an illegal malt beverage at his friend who opened the can and swallowed the entire contents before taking another breath.

"That baldheaded clown will appreciate me when I wipe every gook off the face of the earth!" Bobby exclaimed while both young men laughed at the insanity of that statement.

"You really gonna go to Nam?" Johnny asked.

"Like we are going to have a choice, you stupid idiot."

"I know," Johnny said softly while the two teens walked up the hill to the football field.

The duo neared the crest of the hill, Bobby dropped to the ground, rolled to the side of the path and carefully aimed his arm and finger toward an invisible target and fired off one round with his trigger finger in mid air.

"One shot, one kill!" he shouted and stood up again.

"Did ya get him?" Johnny asked while he stood in the path and chuckled at the familiar scene that was unfolding before him.

"Yeah, I got him, but you, you mother fucker, got wasted first!" Bobby yelled and punched his friend in the nose without mercy.

"Damn it, Bobby. What in hell did you do that for?" Johnny cried while the blood trickled onto his black tee shirt.

"Because you were careless and just got killed you damn fool!" Bobby screamed at his friend. "You ever get killed again, you bastard, and I will kill you, too!" he said as tears filled his eyes before he left his friend alone in the middle of the dirt path and stormed onto the football field.

Not a day ever went by that Bobby Dragon did not read everything he could about the horrors of Vietnam. He knew by the time he arrived in the war torn country, all hell would be breaking loose, but he knew he would win the war for all those who lost their lives. He had to…no one else would or could. This was his life's mission.

That is the reason he practiced firing his weapon at still and live targets, every chance he got. That is the reason he camped out at night…alone or with Johnny, stalking every living and breathing thing in the woods, in the middle of the street, or along the rivers and streams that surrounded his small Vermont town of Marblewood. Practice made perfect, his parents always told him. He lived and breathed that motto.

"You gonna join the Marines?" Johnny asked as the two teens neared the bleachers where hundreds of enthusiastic football fans from the opposing team had gathered.

"Is there any other branch of the military either of us want to join?" Bobby asked and smiled.

"No. We both know the answer to that, don't we?" Johnny asked.

"We will be Marines, God damn it, and we will be proud!" Bobby said with his voice raised above the roar of the crowd.

"Did you say you were going to be a Marine?" a slight, dark haired teenager asked Bobby from the third row of seats of the bleachers.

"Yes, Miss, my friend and I are going to be Marines."

"Go ahead you fool, get yourself killed in that God forsaken jungle," a young man yelled from across the stands.

"What do you know about anything?" Bobby yelled as he glanced one more time at the attractive young girl who had spoken to him, initially.

"I was there, asshole and all that's there is death, man!" the man said and got up and boldly made his way through the throngs of football revelers and stood before the two teens from Marblewood.

"You were there?" Bobby and Johnny asked simultaneously.

"Yes, ass-wipe, I was there!" he barked.

"Let me shake your hand!" Bobby cried with admiration and reached out to grab the man's right hand with his own and in an instant mortification swept over him.

"I left my right arm in Nam, you friggin' pansy!" the man shouted hysterically.

"Oh my God. I am so sorry," Bobby said and without thinking grabbed this veteran's soldier issue, trademark olive green jacket and then wrapped his arms around the man. Both, the veteran and Bobby fell to the ground. Bobby remained in a heap, on the ground, while the Vietnam veteran sprinted to his feet with the grace of a gazelle.

"You ever touch me again, you son of a bitch and I will kill you with my left hand!" the man yelled and marched away from the crowd that was now totally silent. All the members of the football teams stopped, calling 'time-out', to watch this display as well.

"I only wanted to thank you!" Bobby yelled and ran after the soldier who was marching double time to get away from the crowd.

"Listen, you punk," the man said and grabbed Bobby by the scruff of his neck. "Stay away from me and stay away from Nam!" he ordered. "You will be lucky if you come home nearly in one piece like me," he said continued to walk away.

"Leave him alone!" a small voice cried from nearby, from behind Bobby and Johnny who had just joined this stranger at the bottom of the hill where the red Chevy convertible was parked.

"Leave my brother alone!" the dark haired girl cried; the same girl who had captured Bobby's eye only moments before.

"Tell your damn brother I want to talk to him!" Bobby yelled and opened the trunk of his car and took out his rifle and aimed it at the retreating veteran.

The veteran in the olive green military jacket stopped, turned around and marched toward the loaded rifle.

"Go ahead, ass-wipe. Shoot me. You think I give a God damn?" he yelled at the same time the handicapped veteran reached out and snatched the rifle from Bobby's hand before he could blink an eye.

"You ever point a weapon at any man, woman or child and you better make sure you kill them...one shot...one kill," the man said sternly and glared into Bobby's defiant eyes.

"You were a Marine, huh?" Bobby asked softly.

"Ya, punk I will always be a Marine!" he said proudly.

Bobby brazenly reached out and took the weapon from the veteran's hand and walked back to the trunk of his car, put the weapon away and closed the trunk lid.

"Come on Olivia," the veteran said. "We have a long walk home."

"Please let us give you a ride," Bobby pleaded. "It would be an honor to have a Marine ride in my car," he said honestly.

"You gonna make my sister walk?" the veteran growled.

"No, of course not. Let me start again. I would love to have a Marine ride in my car and his beautiful sister ride in the front seat with me," Bobby stated as a matter of fact.

"That's better son," the veteran said, who was no more than four years older than either teen insinuating he was ancient. Technically he was, he knew in his heart and soul. The two years he spent in Vietnam aged him more than thirty years, he swore. He lived to die he told himself every morning. He prayed today would be the day to die.

The foursome rode off into the afternoon sunshine with the convertible top down, with the wind and warmth from the heavens guiding them along.

Bobby woke from this aspiration in a cold sweat as he always did when he dreamt of days long ago. He rose from the double bed and once again took a hot shower. He noted the time was only five o'clock, not even time for the nightly news while he scrubbed his body from head to toe to relax.

He dressed in clean blue jeans and another dark tee shirt and left the hotel to get something to eat in a nearby café. Once he finished his BLT sandwich and two cups of coffee, he strolled along the sidewalk and sat down on a park bench. His mind wandered back to the day he met his sweet Olivia and her brother, former Marine Sergeant Richard Bennett.

"After stopping for snacks and two more six packs of beer, Bobby, Johnny, Olivia and Richard rode in the 1963 Chevy convertible to what was known by the local folk in town as The Quarry. The Quarry was a vast marble encompassed gorge that was filled with water. No one knew whether the stone pit was bottomless or not. No one ever dared to find out how deep it really was.

"After three beers apiece, the three males got acquainted while Olivia sat quietly by, her eyes steadfastly glued to Bobby, the whole time.

"You two are from Centerville?" Johnny asked to break the awkward silence that was common among new found friends.

"Yes, we walked to the game. Our family has one car, but it's in the shop," Richard said knowing that was a lie. He couldn't afford to register the vehicle and in reality, it was parked in their garage at their small, run-down, house.

"I work at a local greenhouse," Richard added for the sake of nothing else to say. "I am not much use to anybody, but the old guy who owns the shop feels sorry for me, I guess, so he hired me to tend to his plants and trees."

"Stop saying that!" Olivia screamed. "You are so important to so many people and me most of all. I am sick of you saying you are no good…no good to anybody."

"Yeah, sis, I'm sorry. I keep forgetting to keep those thoughts to myself."

"Can you tell me more about yourselves?" Bobby asked with intense interest.

"I went to Centerville High and graduated. Went to Nam and served two tours and came home a cripple," Richard said.

"There is a lot more to my brother's story that he will tell. If he won't tell it, I will!" Olivia exclaimed.

"Don't!" Richard warned his sister.

"No, Richard. I am proud of you and I want the whole world to know about you!"

"I am warning you, Olivia," Richard said.

"Well, then, Richard, you tell them or I will and I might not get the story right, so you better tell it like it was," she warned while glaring at her brother with eyes of fire.

"Please tell us about the time you spent in Nam, if you can," Bobby invited.

"I will not talk about it to you or anyone else," Richard said without hesitation. Just heed my advice and stay away from there. It is hell on earth. There is no other way to describe it. But, I will say, I left a whole man and now I am a deformed freak," he said and got up from the ground and walked to the edge of the ravine below.

"Richard, you are a sweet, gentle man. You are my brother and nothing or nobody will ever change that," Olivia finally said after standing beside her only sibling.

"I worried about my brother the whole time he was gone," Olivia said. "I prayed day and night that he would come home. I could never go through that again," she said without hesitation.

"You could, if you had someone special to wait for, couldn't you?" Bobby asked.

"No. I will never fall in love with anyone who goes off to war," Olivia said and walked back to the car, got in the front seat and slammed the door shut.

Bobby was brought back to the present moment in time. The reality of the night while he continued to savor the stillness of the darkness on the park bench in Phoenix. After another few minutes he slowly rose from the wooden seat and walked back to his hotel without thinking about his friend, Johnny, Richard or Olivia until he once again fell into a deep, fitful sleep in his lonely hotel room that night.

OLIVIA
1970

"Bobby, sweetheart," Olivia whispered in his ear while they lay together, as one, in their bed on the night before he was to go back to Vietnam for his second tour of duty.

Sadly, Bobby was sound asleep and never heard what Olivia wanted so desperately, to tell him in her one moment of weakness.

Bobby left for Vietnam the next morning and Olivia would never have the courage to tell him the about the secret she held in her heart and in her belly.

Robert, Bobby, Dragon arrived at the landing zone near Quang Ngai and resumed his profession as one of the most respected Marine snipers the Corps had ever known.

"Are you going to tell him?" the older woman asked her daughter.
"I tried, Mama, but he's gone now, so I'll wait until he comes home. Why make him worry?" she asked with good sense and reason.
"You should have told him before he left?" the woman scolded her daughter.

"No, he has enough on his mind now. He has his men to worry about and he will think I did this on purpose."

"He has a right to know, Olivia and you know as well as I did, you did get pregnant on purpose!" her mother insanely screamed at her only daughter.

"I will tell him when the time is right," Olivia said.

"It's a good thing your brother had enough sense not to have any brats!" the mother continued. "He is a much better man, than your Daddy was! He got killed in that damn car accident and I had to raise you two brats all by myself!" the enraged woman screeched incoherently.

"Well, Mama, how is Richard a better man that Papa was? Just because he doesn't have any children, yet!" Olivia screamed at her mother.

"Yet? What do you mean, yet? Who would want to marry your brother now with his arm missing?"

"Mama, you are crazy just like Papa said!" Olivia yelled and began to cry hysterically. If I didn't know better, I would say Papa died in that accident so he wouldn't have to come home to you!"

"No, Olivia, Papa died in that car accident for another reason," Richard yelled at his mother, in Olivia's defense. "Papa died in that accident because he was working two jobs to help support our family and so you could be treated for your damn insanity!" Richard yelled and rose his left arm as if to strike his mother, but didn't. "He fell asleep at the wheel!"

"Oh, you always defended your father!" the woman screamed.

"You're crazier than a 'shit-house' rat, Mother!" Richard bellowed and stormed out of the house.

"You'll see who's crazy, Richard! Olivia's having Bobby's baby and that brat will be as crazy as Olivia, herself is and I am, too!" she screamed and began to throw every dish from the cupboard on the floor before Olivia ran from the house in a hysterical state of panic.

"Richard!" Olivia yelled while running down the dirt driveway to catch up to her brother. Several moments later she ran into her brother's lone arm while she cried hysterically until her brother could calm her down.

"It's okay, Olivia," Richard said softly while the duo walked to an open meadow, close by.

"What if she's right, Richard? What if the baby is as crazy as I am and mother is?"

"Olivia, there is only one crazy person in that house and she is making an ass of herself again by busting up the house. I am going to have her committed to an institution, but I just need to know how to go about doing that," he added thoughtfully.

"Ask Judge Connors," Olivia suggested while wiping tears from her eyes.

"I will call him from the gas station. Come on, walk with me and we will get a soda, too," he encouraged while he helped his little sister to her feet before heading to town.

Olivia and Richard's mother was hospitalized that next day and neither Olivia or Richard ever saw her again.

Several long months later, Olivia sat with her precious dark haired little girl all that night. She rocked her to sleep, cradled her in her arms and whispered how much she loved her and had to let her go…for her own good.

"I really am crazy, Livy," Olivia whispered through her tears. "I always see and hear things," she added softly while rubbing the baby's plump little cheeks with her finger. "I know I won't be a good mother, sweetheart, so I have to let someone help you grow into a beautiful little girl and woman," she added while her tears caressed the baby's soft, pink blanket.

Olivia left the warmth of her house on a night that a blizzard of biblical per portions raged across the Northeast at the same time Bobby Dragon lay in the darkness of the humid jungle…lying in wait…one shot…one kill.

The entire time Bobby was in Vietnam for this tour, he had not received one letter or one card from the woman he loved and now there was no hope that he ever would as Olivia left the earth to float among the stars and moon.

The only communication he received concerning anyone from that small town was a special notification of Olivia's death by the Red Cross and because of the extenuating circumstances Bobby was allowed to leave Vietnam to attend her funeral.

Richard met Bobby at the funeral for their beloved Olivia, but sadly, Richard never mentioned the baby he had sent away to a foster home just that afternoon. Richard also neglected to mention any reason that Olivia might have ended her own life.

"Where is your mother?" Bobby asked Richard after the funeral that was attended by only themselves.

"She was too ill to attend," Richard said sparing any details about her true whereabouts in the mental hospital.

"Well, please tell her how sorry I am," Bobby said as fresh tears stung his eyes.

"I will," Richard lied.

"Oh, by the way, Bobby," Richard began. "I want you to know how much Olivia loved you."

"If she loved me, then why in hell did she kill herself!" he screamed at the grieving brother.

"Only Olivia knows that," Richard said knowing the innocent young woman truly believe her mother all those years. She believed she would become an insane creature like the woman who gave birth to her, Richard knew.

"I loved her with my whole heart and soul, Richard. I wanted to marry her and have a family," Bobby said and burst into tears while he walked away from the brother of his dearly beloved Olivia for the last time.

The day after her funeral, Bobby went back for another tour of Vietnam and then came back, stateside and finished his career without ever going to that sleepy hollow again.

The Reunion
2003

"Your truck's ready, sir" the ancient mechanic told Bobby after the trucker re-entered the garage, after grabbing a quick bite to eat at a local diner.

"Good, I have to get moving. Time's a'wasting!" Bobby said as he paid the bill.

"I'm sorry it took me two days to get the parts to fix the air conditioner," the mechanic added.

"That's okay. I needed some rest anyway," Bobby said honestly.

"Don't you have to get your load delivered on time?" the man asked.

"Oh, the people I work for are very understanding about that sort of thing," Bobby said mysteriously.

"What ya hauling?" the old man asked.

"Weapons," Bobby said truthfully.

"Illegal weapons?" the man continued without batting an eye.

"Well, for the average citizen they would be."

"You hauling for the government?"

"Yes," Bobby responded.

"You got a magnificent trailer, there," the elderly man said as he gazed upon the graphic design of the Vietnam Wall depicted on the side.

"Yes, it speaks for itself, doesn't it?" Bobby asked while he brushed some imaginary dirt from the sheet metal and focused on one name. A name of which he gently caressed the letters with his fingertips. A name of a friend who belonged to the voice that shouted during his nights of torment while he tried to sleep. The voice that shouted, "Bring me home."

"It sure does. I gather you were in Nam?" the old-timer asked.

"Yeah, for a few years," Bobby responded modestly.

"Yeah kill anyone?"

"One or two of the enemy," Bobby said and got inside the cab before the conversation could become more involved. One thing Bobby never did was lie. He might avoid details in his descriptions of his war-heroics, but he never lied about them.

"Well, the air-conditioner is all set and you shouldn't have any more trouble with it."

"Thanks for getting this job done for me so quickly," Bobby said and bid the old man farewell while he hurried on his way, west.

Speeding along Interstate 10 moments later, he called his 'connections' in California and notified them he was, once again, heading to the usual rendevous point at Camp Pendleton Marine Base.

Several miles down the Interstate his radiator overheated and air conditioning unit once again shut down while anti-freeze gushed from a radiator hose that the mechanic neglected to reattach securely.

"Damn son of a bitch!" Bobby swore while he eased his big-rig to the side of the lonesome highway and noticed a hitch hiker not a half a mile up the highway.

"What in hell would anyone be hitch hiking in the fucking desert?" Bobby asked himself while he eyed the stranger who appeared to be walking toward his truck from a great distance away.

The sun continued to bake the earth and his body while he opened the hood in an attempt to cool the engine and coolant sufficiently to inspect the situation and reattach the hose and clamp while he kept one eye on the approaching stranger.

The unknown male continued to come closer to the rig and Bobby instinctively got his assault rifle from the back of the cab, shoved a magazine into the chamber and watched the older man weakly limp closer.

Bobby noticed this man appeared to have only one arm. The old army jacket he wore seemed to have one sleeve that hung loosely, flapping on the right side of this aging man's body while he approached the tractor trailer.

Bobby watched this man stagger toward his truck. A mere twenty feet in front of the truck the man collapsed to the ground in a heap. The knapsack he had on his back spilled open and poured the entire contents, his worldly possessions, strewn across the melting highway.

Bobby laid is rifle on the front seat of this truck and ran to the stranger's aid.

"Hey, buddy, you okay?" he asked the man who had fainted from exhaustion and the sweltering heat of the afternoon sun.

"Shit, this poor bastard will die if I don't get him out of the sun," Bobby said out loud, opened the door to his truck and carefully picked the injured man up in his arms, as a child, and gently laid him inside. Bobby climbed inside and loosened the man's clothes and poured some water on his face and clothes.

"Damn it," Bobby swore. "I gotta get this damn air-conditioner to work."

Bobby jumped outside the truck and knew the engine and coolant was still blistering hot, but without thought of himself, he grabbed his screw driver, opened the clamp while hot anti-freeze burned his hands. Seconds later he forced the clamp and radiator hose over the nozzle, tightened the clamp while his hands were burned by the scalding coolant without mercy.

"There, that should fix it!" he screamed while blisters formed on his hands and arms.

Bobby grabbed some bottled water and poured it over his hands and arms, fruitlessly, to ease the pain that seared every fiber of the nerve endings in his hands and arms before climbing back inside the truck. Bobby turned the key in the ignition and started the massive truck, while flesh from his fingers peeled away from his hands. The engine roared to life and Bobby flipped the switch to the air-conditioning unit and a blast of arctic air quickly filled the cab. Bobby collapsed against the front seat, beside the stranger who had yet to stir.

Moments later, with hands still throbbing from the pain and welts forming where the flesh remained, Bobby struggled to open the cooler he had in the back, sleeper section of his cab. Without regard for his own injuries, Bobby grabbed some ice water and carefully tended to his passenger, gently applying cool compresses from items of clothing he had thrown in the back of his truck. He soaked a tee shirt in the cool water and applied it to the strangers head and neck before the stranger began to regain consciousness.

"Oh, God, I need a drink," the stranger said.

"Yeah, you do," Bobby said and grabbed a glass and scooped some water from the cooler into it and handed it to the stranger.

"Not that fucking shit!" the man shouted. "I need a fucking drink!" he swore in a rage.

"No, this is about all you can handle right now," Bobby said as if speaking to an injured child.

"How the hell do you know what I can handle, fella?" the man yelled angrily.

The man started to leave the confines of the truck and Bobby grabbed his coat at the same time he noticed the name printed on the tattered army jacket.

"You ever touch me again, you damn ass-wipe and I will kill you with my left hand!" the man shouted and jumped from the truck.

Bobby froze as if he had been electrocuted by a bolt of lightening. The name, the voice, the threat...

"It couldn't be...it couldn't be," Bobby whispered but remained still as stone in the front seat of his beloved Vietnam Memorial.

The stranger, stumbling across the highway, attempted to retrieve his meager belongings and put them back in his backpack, but once again, fell to the ground.

Livy and Jason
2003

Jason, what's the matter?" Livy asked with deep concern. Her husband had come home from work, the last few days, in an extremely irritable mood, so unlike him. Livy knew it had something to do with the fact she had thrown out the trunk that contained the few items she knew had belonged to her mother...the mother she never knew. The mother who deserted her so long ago.

"Nothing," Jason said and stormed into his computer room and slammed the door shut and locked it behind him.

Jason turned on his computer and once again scanned various websites in search of some clue to the mysterious Vietnam Memorial tractor trailer. He searched through the NIIC, National Intelligence and Information Center for some clue from the license plate he memorized that day. That part was easy, he thought. He had never seen such a meaningful license plate on any vehicle before. The letters, NAMSNIPER said it all, but there was no record anywhere of a license plate registered to any vehicle, not to mention a tractor trailer rig with that identification. Jason was frantically trying to locate that vehicle. He knew...he knew who that man was...he knew. He had to find him before it was too late.

"Jason McAllister, open this door immediately!" Livy demanded.

Jason wearily rose from his seat that he had nearly become attached to for the last few days and opened the door.

"If you don't tell me what's wrong, Jason, I am leaving!" she screamed at her husband.

"Where are you going to go?" Jason asked quietly.

"Oh, is that all you have to say? Not, oh, sweetheart, I'm sorry I have been such an ugly bastard lately and please forgive me?" Livy yelled.

"Livy, I can't tell you yet. It is something I am working on and I may not be able to find the answer and I don't want to get your hopes up," Jason calming explained and held out his arms for his very pregnant wife.

"Get my hopes up? Get my hopes up about what?" she asked and began to cry.

"I think I have found your father. I met him the other day, but I can't find him now!"

"You think you found my father?" Livy asked sarcastically. "I have no father or mother Jason, remember?"

"No, Livy, you have a father. Everyone has or had a father and mother at one time," he tried to explain while he caressed her tear stained face.

"Just how have you come to the conclusion you know who my father might be and where he was or is?"

"I read those papers and letters that were in that trunk a long time ago and when I ran across this man laying in the highway in the desert, he told me his name and I remember I heard that name before and I know it was in those letters."

"Oh, so you found some drunk laying in the highway and of course he would be my father, right?" Livy screamed again, pulled herself away from her husband, and stormed out of the room.

"You don't understand!" Jason yelled while he followed his wife into the living room.

"Tell me then," Livy demanded with her hands on her swollen hips.

"He wasn't drunk…he was asleep."

"Oh, of course. Every sober man falls asleep in the middle of the desert highway."

"He had been practicing his sniper techniques, I guess and he fell asleep. Do you know snipers wait in one positions for hours, if not days without moving for their target?" he asked insanely of his wife who wouldn't have a clue as to what he was referring to.

"Oh, Jason, you've gone off the deep end. I'm leaving until you get some help!" Livy said and left the room.

Jason's cell phone rang and Livy ran to answer it before Jason could.

"Hi Livy. Is Jason there?"

"Yes, Derek my husband is here, but I won't be," she said and left the cell phone on the table. "Your partner, Trooper Derek Anderson wants to talk to you," Livy said sarcastically and sat on the couch beside the phone.

"Jason, what's wrong?" Derek asked.

"I've been a real bastard for the last few days and I was trying to explain to Livy what I'm trying to do and unfortunately, my nerves have gotten the best of my disposition and I am frantic."

"Well, your wife needs you, not some father who might not even exist, Jason, so you better try and make peace with Livy. She needs you now more than ever. She is having your baby any time. That's all that's important now."

"I know, Derek. I'll make it up to her, I swear, but I've been freaking out, here. Can you imagine...Robert Dragon...the Namsniper could be her father?" Jason said with his chest swollen with pride.

"Jason, I hate to disappoint you, but I can't find a damn thing on that plate or tractor trailer," Jason's partner confirmed.

"I know, Derek. I can't either. It's like I was dreaming the whole thing. It's like it never happened and there is no such vehicle or person."

"Well, you know there is such a person. Gunnery Sergeant Robert Dragon does exist, but his whereabouts must be either top secret or he is using an alias."

"He might be. He was one hell of a soldier. Do you think he might be working for the government?" Jason asked while Livy listened intently to this mysterious conversation.

"I bet he is. I wonder where he would have been headed?" Derek asked. "You said he was headed West?"

"Yes, he was," Jason said.

"Well, let me work on it and you work on your marriage and take care of your wife," Derek said and hung up.

Jason hung disconnected the call and held his arms out for his wife who fell into them and began to cry as they eased themselves on the couch.

Jason McAllister told Livy Bennett-McAllister what he knew about Gunnery Sergeant Robert Dragon…the Namsniper…his hero…every Marines hero.

Bobby and The Stranger
2003

"Come on, buddy, let me help you up," Bobby said as he helped the one armed man back inside the cab of his tractor trailer, as best he could with his severely burned hands and arms.

Once the man was inside the truck, Bobby went back outside and collected the few meager belongings the stranger owned.

The stranger looked at Bobby and noticed his hands. "Jesus, you need to get to the doctors," the man exclaimed in total honesty.

"Yeah, well, for some reason I haven't been able to leave this Godforsaken spot for a while," he said sarcastically at the stranger he knew so well, but to whom he did not reveal that fact.

"Well, let me out and get going," the stranger said, but made no effort to leave the coolness of the cab.

"I might need help driving this bitch. If you haven't noticed my hands are not what they were a few minutes ago," Bobby growled at the man who sat beside him.

"Like I can drive with one arm," the man sparred with his new acquaintance.

"You always did have a foul mood about you," Bobby said and began to shift the massive truck with every ounce of stamina he had. "You always did feel sorry for yourself because you lost your fucking arm in Nam, didn't you?" Bobby spat.

"What did you say?"

"You heard me, didn't you or have you lost your damn hearing as well!" Bobby yelled while pain seared through his hands and arms as the truck proceeded down the interstate.

"Who the fuck are you?" the stranger asked.

"None of your damn business, that's who."

"Just shut the fuck up and let me drive. I need to get these damn hands looked at," he said and remained silent until he approached the exit to the next town.

"What happened to your hands?" the stranger asked quietly.

"I just had this truck serviced and the mechanic didn't tighten the hose clamp, evidently, and it came off. I was in such a hurry to get you out of the heat and inside where it was cool, I rushed to put the hose back on, with the fucking coolant spewing all over the place and on my damn hands, that's what?"

"I'm sorry about your hands," the stranger said sincerely and looked out the window and admired the beauty of the stark no-man's land that passed by.

"They'll heal," Bobby said without emotion as he eased the truck into the hospital parking lot and got out.

"Stay here and get some rest," Bobby ordered his companion. "I'll be out as soon as I can," he said and left the truck idling with the air conditioner on.

The stranger was and never had been one to disrespect anyone's property and even though he was beyond curious as to who this man was, he didn't violate any possessions in the truck. Within moments he was asleep and nightmares he always had once again forced themselves into his subconscious.

"Mr. Dragon, you have got to let your hands heal before you consider driving your tractor trailer," an elderly physician warned Bobby.

"I have places to go and people to see," he whined with self pity.

"How do you plan on shifting your truck?" the doctor continued as he wrote out a prescription for pain medication for his patient.

"Just give me some drugs and I will be on my way," Bobby ordered.

"I will give you a few day's supply, but I can't stress enough the fact you need to get some rest and let your hands heal."

"I will be at my destination in another day and then I will rest," he promised with every intention of doing just that.

"Here you go," the doctor said and handed Bobby a prescription.

"Thanks, Doc," Bobby said and left the emergency room.

Bobby opened the truck's door and noticed his passenger was sleeping, peacefully, at the moment and he hated to disturb him. He watched this man while he slept and wondered what his life had been like for the last thirty years. He knew in his heart, his life had been a living hell…much like his own.

Bobby started the big rig's engine without waking his passenger and drove a few miles to a pleasant looking hotel, parked the truck, and made a reservation for a large room with two double beds for several days. He knew he couldn't continue on with his trip in his condition and he knew his friend wouldn't be able to shift the gears, either. He also realized maybe these whole series of events had happened for a reason. A reason he had yet to realize. Bobby was a man who truly believed in fate and he now wondered why fate had delivered this man into his life at this time.

Bobby reached for his cell phone and called his contacts at Camp Pendleton, informing them he would be delayed a for a few more days and explained why. As he expected, there was no problem with his time schedule. The weapons he was hauling could wait for a few more days before they were delivered. Bobby disconnected the call and continued to watch this man sleep for a few more minutes.

"Come on buddy," Bobby said, finally. "I have a nice room for us for a few days and I think we both deserve a good meal, don't you?" he asked the man who struggled to waken from his deep sleep.

"I don't have any money," the man painfully admitted.

"Did I ask you for any money?" Bobby asked while he gathered his seabag and shaving kit from the back of the cab.

"No, but I'm not a charity case," the man growled with pride.

"I owe you one," Bobby said and smiled.

"You owe me one, what?"

"For a six pack of beer," Bobby said and smiled again.

"A six pack of beer?"

"Yeah; I guess you have forgotten all about that, huh?"

"Who the hell are you?"

"Does the name Bobby Dragon mean anything to you?"

Shock and disbelief consumed this man's face and body while he starred intently at the man who had once been a young, smart-ass kid. A kid who had done what he said he would do. He made a name for himself as one of the most highly decorated Marines the United States had ever known. This man who picked him up from the middle of the desert was a man he admired more than anyone he had ever known. With tears in his eyes, Richard Bennett looked into the eyes of the man who had literally saved his life that day.

"Bobby!" Richard said as a tear cascaded down his cheek. "Bobby Dragon!"

With bandaged hands, Bobby reached out and hugged the man who had been his friend. The brother of the woman he loved. The brother of the woman he had loved and lost. Each man shed more tears while they embraced than they had allowed themselves in over thirty years.

Livy and Jason
2003

Livy cradled her newborn daughter, Sarah, in her arms while the proud father looked on, with love and fear in his heart.

"I'm afraid," Jason admitted to his wife. "We have tried to have a baby for so long and now that she's here, I am scared to death. That was bad enough, but now they say her little heart is not fully developed and will need a transplant."

"I know," Livy said as she frowned, but forced herself to smile at her daughter. Livy didn't want any negative feelings to surround her newborn baby. "Knowing we are responsible for her, forever, is a frightening thought, but I know you will be a wonderful father and we will get through this together, as a family."

"I guess I have plenty of experience with raising children, don't I?" he said and laughed.

"Yes, you have four younger brothers and two sisters you helped raise, so this should be a piece of cake."

"I know, but I could always threaten them into behaving," Jason said and laughed. "I always told them if they didn't behave I would tell our parents they broke the cookie jar...mom's favorite cookie jar, while she and Dad were bowling.

"You broke the cookie jar, Jason," Livy said.

"I know, but who were our parents going to believe...them or me?"

"Knowing your parents, they would not have believed you!" Livy said and laughed just as Jason's parents entered the hospital room to see their first grandchild.

"We were just talking about you and Dad," Livy said and smiled wickedly at her In-laws.

"We heard," Mrs. McAllister said. "Jason, we always knew you broke the cookie jar," she added.

"You did?" Jason asked

"Yes, of course we did," Mr. McAllister responded.

"How did you know?" their son asked.

"Jason, you were the only child who had airplane glue on their hands when we got home from bowling that night, so in light of the fact you tried to repair the broken pieces, and not very well at that, it didn't take a detective to figure it out, my dear," Mrs. McAllister said.

"Oh," Jason said while blushing from head to toe.

"Well, now that, that is over and done with, let me hold my granddaughter," Mrs. McAllister said before cradling the little bundle of joy in her arms.

"Any more information about this mysterious Robert Dragon you're trying to locate?" Mr. McAllister asked his son.

"No, Dad. It's like it never happened. It's like I dreamt the whole thing."

"Maybe you did?" Livy asked with a touch of anger in her voice. "I really wish he would stop investigating this. I am not interested in finding some long lost father, now," Livy said. "I want you to let it go, Jason," Livy ordered.

"I guess I should. There is no sense in stirring anything up after all these years, I guess," he added somberly.

Bobby and Richard
2003

Bobby and Richard made themselves at home in the large, comfortable hotel room. Both men traveled light, so their belongings didn't take long to store away in the closet and dresser drawers.

"Let's get a bite to eat and then maybe see a movie." Bobby suggested to his old friend.

"Let's get a bite to eat and maybe a few drinks," Richard began. "A movie is the last thing I want to see or do tonight. I have so many things I have to tell you.; confess to you, Bobby and now that I have the chance, I don't want it to slip away again."

"Okay, Richard, but what could you have to tell me; confess to me?"

"Let's eat and get drunk first," Richard begged.

"You will have to be drunk to talk to me?"

"About this, yes!"

"Okay, well let's get going. I have a feeling I am not going to like what you have to tell me. Am I right?"

"I guess you could say that," Richard admitted while he undressed to take a shower before they went out.

While Richard prepared the water in the bathroom, Bobby noticed the man had hardly any other clothes than the dirty ones he wore.

"I'm not going anywhere with you looking like you do and smelling like your old clothes do, Richard."

"Well, what in hell do you expect me to wear...this bath towel?" Richard asked while he strolled and strutted out of the bathroom with the large bath towel provocatively draped around his body.

"You're a fucking asshole!" Bobby said and fell on the bed, laughing like he hadn't laughed in years.

"Oh, Bobby...make love to me!" Richard screeched and seductively approached the man who remained laying on the bed, howling in a fit of laughter.

"Get away from me you freak!" Bobby yelled and sprinted off the bed, injuring his hands in the process.

"God damn it!" Bobby yelled and waved his injured hands in the air.

"Hey, I'm sorry," Richard said and stopped his fooling around. "I was just kidding with you."

"I know. It's not your fault," Bobby admitted.

"Look get a shower and you and I are going to get haircuts, some new clothes and go out on the town!" Bobby said, excitement in his voice.

"Okay...you have to pay!" Richard reminded his friend.

"Richard, if you mention money again, I will cut your balls off," Bobby said. "I haven't spent a dime of my money in so long, I have no idea who much money I have. The government pays my way, so knock off the shit about money, okay?"

"The government pays your way?" Richard asked.

"Yes, Richard. I transport goods for the military. They pay my way."

"Sounds like a job I would like," Richard admitted.

"Well, maybe I could use a partner. I'm not getting any younger and it gets lonely on the road...but NOT that lonely," Bobby said while he watched Richard begin a Hula dance for him, again, with the big white bath towel as his grass skirt.

Both men finished their showers, rented a car from the hotel, found a barber that was open, got haircuts and their faces shaved, found an expensive men's store and bought several pair of blue jeans, several dress shirts, tee shirts, underwear, new shoes and several new jackets.

Both men rode around the streets with no particular destination in mind while they continued to talk.

"You know, you never told me what you did in Vietnam that Olivia was so proud of you for, Richard."

"It was nothing, Bobby. Nothing more than anyone else did."

"I know you better than that. What really happened to your arm?"

Richard hesitated for several minutes before he began his story while Bobby patiently waited for the obviously distressed man to begin.

"We were trapped in a bunker. There were probably ten of us packed in there and we spotted some VC nearly on top of us. We had all run out of ammo, but I had one grenade in my flak jacket pocket. I took it out, pulled the pin and dropped the God damn thing. I bent down to pick it up and get rid of it before it blew us all to kingdom come and just as I picked it up, it exploded in my hand. Unfortunately, two other men died because of my mistake. I only lost an arm. So, I don't know how in hell Olivia thinks I am some sort of damn hero. Two men died because of me."

"How many of the VC died, Richard?" Bobby asked.

"They all did," Richard said. "The four VC who were nearly on top of us died, too."

"So, you lost your arm and two other poor souls from your unit died, Richard, but you saved seven other men's lives including your own. You know as well as I do if the VC hadn't been killed, they would have killed you all. You said yourself you were all out of ammunition."

"I have had to live with that mistake every day, Bobby. I would have traded my life for one of those boys any day and you know it."

"Yes, I do know it, Richard, but that was not what God had in mind for you. He had other plans for you. You have to trust me on that. I have to remind myself of that fact now and then, too," Bobby whispered and continued driving through the city streets.

Several hours later, both Richard and Bobby entered a fine dining establishment and made themselves comfortable at a table in the corner, away from the three piece band that played soothing music, for the benefit of the diners.

"Well, I think I'm going to order a thick steak, but I'm not sure if I'll be able to cut it," Bobby admitted, looking at his injured hands.

"I live with that dilemma every day," Richard mentioned.

"I realize that, now. I apologize for suggesting that you simply feel sorry for yourself for no reason."

"I do the best I can and deal with my handicap the best way I know how."

"How is that?" Bobby asked.

"I drink all the time."

"Does that really help anything?"

"No, but I don't care about much of anything else. I just drink until I pass out."

"I'm sorry, Richard. I truly am."

"Do they really hurt a lot?" Richard asked referring to Bobby's injured hands with concern in am attempt to change the subject from his drinking problem.

"Yes, but this medicine helps," Bobby said while he took another pain pill with his glass of water while the waiter waited to take their order.

"I will have a steak, chef's salad, order of onion rings and Budweiser," Bobby said.

"Make that two?" Richard echoed. "We can try to eat that," he added and laughed.

"Yeah, I have to hold the beer like a baby," Bobby whined.

"How did you take a shower?" Richard asked, noting his bandages had not gotten wet.

"Not very well. I just wrapped my hands in the two shower caps that were in the stall and did what I could. I will let you lather me up, next time!" Bobby said and howled with laughter.

"Like hell!" Richard exclaimed.

"You were the one doing the damn Hula," Bobby said out loud while other customers eyed them warily.

"Honestly, Richard, tell me what you've been doing all these years," Bobby asked while they both struggled to eat their salads, onion rings and drink their beers. "God, I feel like a damn child," Bobby complained while he attempted to hold his silverware with both hands heavily bandaged before Richard could respond.

"Now you know how I have felt all these years?" Richard said honestly.

"Yeah, I guess you're right," Bobby admitted.

"You're right, of course. I do feel sorry for myself. There is no one else to," Richard said while he stabbed the piece of steak with his fork, surrendering to any manners he might have wanted to display in public.

"Hell, this thing will have mold growing on it before I get to eat it," he said while he chewed a piece of meat off without concern of what other patrons might have thought while they watched him eat.

"I guess that's about the only way to eat this while it's still warm," Bobby admitted while he speared his own steak and sunk his teeth into it and broke a piece of meat off to eat.

"Animals, we are," Richard said while both men laughed at each other for their lack of manners; at the fact, also, that they didn't care what anyone else thought.

The two men enjoyed their meal and drank several more beers and allowed the waiter to remove their plates and silverware before Bobby asked Richard what it was he had to confess.

"This isn't the place to talk about that," Richard said while nervously drumming the fingers of his left hand on the table.

"Well, damn it, where is the place to discuss what you have to say?" Bobby asked with anger edging his voice.

"Come on," Richard said while standing up from the table. "Outside, away from the crowds," he added while walking away.

Bobby grabbed the check, paid the bill, followed Richard outside and got inside the rental car and sat facing his passenger.

"Spill it!" Bobby demanded.

Richard turned and in the darkness of the night, he could see the outline of a man he had known as a teenager, who had grown into a man he admired more than any man he had ever known. Richard took a deep breath and began his story.

"Bobby, you never met my mother did you?"

"No, Richard you know that. Olivia and you, for that matter, never allowed me to come to your house."

"There was a reason for that, Bobby."

"I assumed that," Bobby said sarcastically. "I guessed I wasn't good enough to meet your mother. I assumed Olivia was ashamed of me."

"Bobby, that is as far from the truth as possible. Our mother was a damn 'nut-case'! She was insane, most of the time. We kept everyone away from her. She would go off the 'deep end' at the drop of a hat. We never knew when she would explode, so we just kept everyone away."

"Why didn't you or Olivia ever tell me? Was it she was afraid I would run away or leave her because you had a lunatic for a mother?"

"Well, I guess that pretty much sums it up," Richard said as a tear trickled from his eye.

"Well, it's nice to know you and your sister had so much confidence in me. It's nice to know you didn't trust me enough or reveal such a personal secret."

"I know, Bobby and I'm sorry."

"Well, I'm glad to know you thought so little of me," Bobby added sorrowfully.

"It wasn't that, Bobby. We were ashamed of her."

"Well, maybe she needed help?"

"She did, Bobby and the reason she wasn't at Olivia's funeral was because I did have her committed to an mental hospital. I had finally had enough of her shit and she has been hospitalized ever since. Frankly, I'm not even sure if she is still alive or not and I really don't care."

"Speaking of Olivia's funeral, are you ever going to tell me why she took her own life, you fucker?" Bobby yelled at the mournful, broken man who sat beside him in the car.

"Yes, that is what I am going to tell you and more," Richard said, his eyes averting the eyes of his friend.

"Well, tell me!" Bobby yelled more loudly.

"Olivia was afraid she was going to be insane like our mother, Bobby. Our mother convinced her she would become insane too, over time, as she aged."

"You were both intelligent human beings. Did either of you really believe that shit?" Bobby screamed.

"She did, Bobby. She really did."

"So she killed herself to prevent herself from becoming insane?"

"I guess so."

"Well, if she did take her life only because she thought she would one day be crazy, I guess she really was!" Bobby exclaimed, his body shaking from rage.

"No, Bobby, that wasn't the real reason." Richard said and sighed heavily and began to weep.

"Well, ass-wipe, tell me what the hell the reason was!"

Richard hesitated for several painful minutes to compose himself.

"You didn't know Olivia was carrying your child when you left for Nam, did you?" Richard finally said and waited for a bandaged fist to start beating him senseless.

"What the hell did you just say?" Bobby said as tears cascaded down his cheeks. "She was pregnant and killed herself?" Bobby yelled through his river of tears.

"No, Bobby. She gave birth, loved the baby, but she was afraid she would be a terrible mother and hurt the baby."

"She had a baby?" Bobby asked in horror at the prospect that he had a child all these years and didn't know it.

'Where the fuck is my baby?" Bobby demanded as rage overcame his sorrow.

"The day of the funeral, she was taken to a foster home."

"You mean to tell me I was right in town…my baby right there and you didn't or wouldn't tell me, you fucking bastard?" Bobby said and indeed stuck his friend with one blow before he screamed in pain from his own injuries.

Bobby bolted from the car and ran over to the passenger's side of the vehicle.

"Open this door you mother fucker, so I can kick the living shit out of you!" Bobby screamed. "I am going to kill you, you bastard!" he yelled more loudly than before.

Richard slowly opened the car door and unsteadily left the car and stood still, waiting for the barrage of blows his friend would inflict on his body, not caring one way or another.

Bobby stood still, looking at the broken man who stood before him, and the two men fell into each other's arms and cried as if their hearts had just been torn from their bodies.

Many long moments later the two men composed themselves and remained eerily silent, each dealing with their own thoughts of the past.

"Bobby, do you want to know what I have been doing ever since Olivia's death?"

"What, Richard; what have you been doing?" Bobby asked sincerely, wiping one last tear from his cheek.

"I have spent every waking moment looking for the baby Olivia had. The baby I sent to a foster home. I have been homeless all these years. I have had to keep on the move to find her."

"Her?" Bobby asked. "She had a baby girl? I have a baby daughter?"

"Well, Bobby, I assume she has grown up some in the last thirty years or so," Richard reminded his friend with a smile.

"Yeah, I guess she is a woman by now."

"Come on, Bobby. Let's go back to the hotel and I'll tell you what I know. What I remember."

"Okay, let's go," Bobby agreed and the duo speed off toward their hotel.

Once they parked the rental car next to the roaming Vietnam Wall on wheels, Richard asked, "Whatever happened to your friend Johnny Blackburn?"

Bobby turned with the expression of a wounded animal on his face before he responded.

Bobby slowly walked to the trailer of the Vietnam War tribute, with Richard following close behind. Bobby reached up and caressed the name on the western panel number 33, line 21 and without speaking showed Richard where his best friend was. Only a name on a wall.

Several moments passed without either man speaking.

"I let him down," Bobby began. "It was my fault. I was supposed to protect him and I let him down," he continued as fresh tears stung his eyes.

"What happened, Bobby?"

"He was a sniper, like me. He was the best man I had. We were watching this make-shift school, filled with teachers and elders. The VC used that school as a staging area and we knew it. It was just he and I that day. We lost two other snipers the day before in a fierce firefight, but I demanded we stay out at this site anyway. Johnny was watching the school from an anthill on the east of the school and I spotted the VC coming from the west. I told him to stay put and I would circle around from the other side. We didn't want to harm any civilians so I thought that was the best plan."

Bobby stopped for a moment while he wiped the tears and perspiration from his face with his clean handkerchief.

"Take your time, Bobby."

Bobby swallowed hard and continued his story.

"Johnny saw two VC coming up from behind me, when I got situated. I knew they were behind me and I was ready, but he didn't know I knew their whereabouts. He jumped up and hollered to me, just as two VC grabbed him from behind and dragged him away!" The two fuckers who were behind me, jumped me, but I fought them off but not before Johnny was gone. They captured Johnny. I heard him screaming as they dragged him away. I will never forget that sound as long as I live, Richard!" Bobby said as tears cascaded down his face.

"Did you ever find him...his body?"

"No, Johnny is listed as MIA...Missing In Action. I let him down. I searched high and low for three weeks. I never found a trace of him. It's like he disappeared off the face of the earth. I will never forgive myself. The rest of our unit came and literally dragged me from that area. They were considering called me AWOL because I hadn't report back to base camp, after telling them Johnny was missing. I was not leaving of my own free will until I found my best friend. I never found him, Richard. I never found him."

Both men remained silent for many long moments, staring at the name on the side of the tractor trailer. The name of Johnny Blackburn.

"Our lives have been nothing but filled with pain, have they?" Bobby finally asked.

"It appears that way. War is hell and any man who says it isn't hasn't ever been there," Richard said.

"I guess we have done the best with what we have been dealt. The cards we've been dealt with," Bobby said.

"Come on, Richard. I want to hear the rest of your story," Bobby said as he put his arm around his friend and both men entered the hotel for the night.

Both men undressed and each crawled under the covers of their double beds, turned off the light, and continued talking. Neither man wanted the other to see his facial expression; their expression of sorrow they each shared.

"You said you have been homeless all these years?" Bobby asked.

"Yes. I haven't had an desire to settle down. Never found anyone who wanted me. You know, the one armed bandit. And I felt I owed it to the baby…well, woman, now, to tell her about her mother and father."

"What do you know about the woman?"

"All I really know is a family from Vermont took her into their home, but that family moved shortly afterward and I never found out their names. You know, back then, secrecy was a big deal. But, what I do remember is that Olivia was insistent that her baby's name be Livy, after her, and never be changed.

'Livy, was the baby's name?" Bobby asked and smiled.

"Yes, so I assume it still is. Of course, she most likely is married now, so any last name, even if I knew it, would have changed."

"Well, now that we are partners, if you want, it might be easier to find her with the use of a vehicle," Bobby said thoughtfully.

"I have looked all over the United States and come up empty," Richard warned.

"Well, I have a laptop computer and maybe we can use that to look from phone records, birth records and marriage certificates," Bobby suggested.

"Do you have access to government files, seems you work for the government?" Richard asked hopefully.

"I do, actually," Bobby confirmed. "Let's get some sleep and we will start looking tomorrow while we head west. I have to get this load delivered."

"Okay, I really am beat. This has been one hell of a day," Richard said and quickly fell asleep while Bobby laid awake for hours. Thinking about a family member he never knew he had and wanted desperately to find her.

"Olivia, you will forever be in my broken heart." he whispered as he drifted into a fitfull sleep.

The next morning the duo packed their belongings into the tractor trailer and after a quick breakfast, headed west down the interstate.

"I am going to stop by the hospital and get these bandages changed," Bobby said. "I think they are somewhat better now and won't need to be padded so much. I can't drive for shit with them like they are now," he added.

"I hope you're right," Richard said as the truck pulled into the hospital parking lot.

"Do you know anything about computers?" Bobby asked while he took the laptop computer from the back of the big rig.

'No, I don't but if you show me what I need to do, I will try to mess with it while you're inside," Richard offered.

"I will get it up and running and show you what you can do," he offered.

Bobby was surprised how quickly Richard caught on to the logistics and mechanics of the computer and within minutes, Richard was surfing the Internet in search of a woman named Livy while Bobby entered the emergency room of the local hospital to have his bandages changed.

A MORTALLY WOUNDED HEART

Upon entering the hospital Bobby heard the nurses speaking about a newborn baby who was in need of a new heart and the alert had gone out in search of a match in order for the baby to survive.

"That poor little thing. She is so small and weak. Do you know if she doesn't get a new heart in a matter of days, she will die," Bobby heard an elderly nurse say to a younger woman.

"May I help you?" the younger nurse asked Bobby.

"Yes, the doctor told me to come back, if I wanted, to get these bandages changed."

"Oh, please follow me. I can take care of those for you," she added and led Bobby into an examining room.

"A baby is sick, huh?" Bobby asked.

"Yes, she is a newborn, but her little heart isn't strong enough for her to survive."

"That's too bad," Bobby said, thinking of the baby he had, but never knew.

The nurse quickly completed the task at hand and Bobby left the hospital, still thinking about the baby who needed a new heart.

Bobby told Richard about the baby in need of a new heart and the duo continued on their journey on the interstate toward California.

Several hours later Richard, frustrated that he was unable to find any woman named Livy, who was approximately thirty years old, anywhere in the United States.

"Maybe she doesn't even live in the United States, Richard," Bobby said with equal disappointment in his heart and soul.

"This is a hopeless case," Richard added. "I never regretted anything more in my whole life than I did surrendering that baby to strangers, Bobby. I know you will never forgive me. Why should you? I have never forgiven myself."

"You did what you thought was right at the time. You were under extreme mental anguish. You just buried your sister, your mother is or was a damn nut case, you were dealing with your own demons of your military experience and you did what you could for the baby. I will never hold you responsible for that. I can only pray she was brought up with loving, caring foster parents."

"Shit! Look at that!" Bobby exclaimed pointing toward the west, with his finger touching the windshield. "Looks like that helicopter is having trouble!"

"Damn! You're right. Looks like it is trying to steady itself and make an emergency landing! Jesus…it's spinning out of control!" Bobby added.

"It's coming down, right in front of us!" Richard exclaimed while Bobby slammed the brakes on to avoid colliding with the small aircraft that was landing in the middle of the deserted highway.

The helicopter, with a red cross on the side, crash-landed in front of the tractor trailer and began to smolder with flames licking the cockpit just as the doors opened and the occupants rushed from the burning wreckage.

Bobby and Richard ran, with fire extinguishers in hand, toward the two men who exited the aircraft and tried in vain to douse the flames.

"There is a cooler in the back that has a heart in it!" one man yelled.

Bobby dropped the fire extinguisher and without a moments hesitation ran to the burning inferno and spotted the red and white cooler. He reached inside the aircraft, with Richard applying what was left of the chemicals inside the second fire extinguisher on Bobby's hands while he grabbed the cooler and within seconds both men ran to the safety of the tractor trailer, just as the helicopter exploded sending debris for more than one hundred yards in all directions.

"Holy mother of God!" the first man yelled. "Are you guys alright?" he asked with deep concern in his voice.

"Yes, we're alright. Are you guys okay?" Bobby asked, ripping the smoldering bandages from his already burned hands.

"We are paramedics, let me take a look at those hands," the first man said.

"There's a medical kit and ice water in the back of the truck," Bobby yelled.

Both men, dressed in appropriate medical uniforms, ran to the vehicle and within moments brought the medical kit and bottles of ice water and began to administer first aid to Bobby's hands.

"Are you guys okay?" Richard asked. "Jesus, your helicopter just crashed. You must have busted your assess!" he said with more tact than he usually displayed.

"Yes, my butt is sore, but it will heal," the first man said. "My name is Jim Benson and this is Terry Connors," he added while tending to the injured trucker.

"Your hands were already burned," Jim added.

"Yeah, I had a busted heater hose and it got me a day or so ago. I just came from the hospital in Red Creek and we were on our way to California."

"You just came from Methodist Hospital in Red Creek?" Terry asked.

"Yes," Bobby said.

"That is where we were going with this heart," Jim said. "There is a little baby that needs it and we have to get there…yesterday!" he added.

"When I was in the emergency room I heard the nurses talking about that baby. We better get this cooler inside the air-conditioning of the truck and get our butts to that hospital," Bobby said and stood up.

"You can't drive now!" Richard said. "God almighty, your hands are toast!"

"I know…can either of you drive a tractor?" Bobby asked hopefully.

"I drove one for nineteen years before I became a medic, so let's roll!" Terry said while everyone gathered up the bottled water, medical kit and red and white Igloo cooler.

Within seconds, all the occupants were secured inside the tractor trailer rig and after several attempts to maneuver the big rig around without getting stuck in the desert sand, the truck was heading east, back from where it came hours before.

While this massive rig barreled down the interstate, Bobby held the cooler in his injured hands and without realizing it he was rocking the cooler in his arms.

"Hush…be still my heart. You will be safe and sound in no time," he whispered to the cooler while tears cascaded down the other three men's cheeks. Bobby might have whispered to the Igloo cooler, that cradled the life saving organ, the baby's heart inside, but his words did not fall on deaf ears.

While maneuvering the big rig east, toward the hospital, Terry radioed the medical facility, using Bobby's CB radio, informing the medical staff of the helicopter crash, but assured the anxiously waiting hospital staff they were on their way with the contents of the cooler.

All four occupants of the tractor trailer quickly exited the vehicle without benefit of leaving the rig in a proper parking space. Bolting inside the emergency room, Richard handed the cooler to a waiting physician who rushed off toward an operating room without as much as a thank you.

"You need to get those hands treated," Terry said and led Bobby toward the registration desk he had left only hours before.

"What have you done to your hands?" a pretty middle-aged nurse asked Bobby Dragon. "You just left here and now you're back and your hands are more severely burned than before. What am I going to do with you?" she asked sternly, but with a smile on her face.

"I just wanted to come back and have you take care of them for me. I wanted to see your smile one more time before I left," he added, flirting shamelessly for the first time in years with any woman.

"Well, I like a man who can USE his hands, so if you want to see me again,"she began. "You better let them heal properly before you ask me out on a date."

Bobby looked at this petite woman, who appeared to be in her mid forties. Her beautiful clear blue eyes and bright dark auburn hair highlighted her fair skin and few freckles that dotted her tiny nose.

"My name is Bobby and your name is...?"

"Mr. Dragon, my name is Rebecca, Becky, Smith and I will be happy to accept your invitation for dinner tonight. You will need someone to help feed you," she added and smiled while she gently led him inside an examination room.

"Well, hot damn...that bastard is putting the make on that woman without even trying!" Richard said and smiled while he and his new friends sat and waited for some news on Bobby's developing romance and the condition of the heart transplant patient.

"He sure is smooth!" Terry said with Jim in total agreement.

"I need to hang with him more often. I need to take some lessons from him. I am sick of being alone," Richard said sadly while he flipped the pages of an old Time magazine without really looking at the pictures or reading the words.

Moments later, Bobby and nurse Smith exited the examination room while the most attentive nurse gently led Bobby, by his elbow, toward a seat in the waiting room. Bobby's hands were totally wrapped in gauze bandages, a pathetic site at best.

"I won't even be able to pee!" Bobby whined, looking for sympathy from the beautiful, small figured, shapely woman.

"I don't know you well enough to help you in that area," she said. "Yet," she added, smiled and walked off.

"God damn, man. What in hell are you wearing for aftershave or what magical spell have you cast on her?" Richard asked.

"I am wearing Olivia's favorite aftershave," he said while lowering his eyes from his former lover's brother.

"Bobby...it is time to move on. She died thirty years ago. You have to move on!"

"What about you, Richard? How long are you going to play the pathetic cripple with one arm?" Bobby asked gently.

"I know; we both have to move on, now!"

Becky Smith came back an hour later and reported there was some positive news about the heart transplant to the anxiously waiting foursome.

"The baby is holding her own and the father would like to meet with you, if you don't mind. He wants to thank you for what you've done," the nurse said while looking at Bobby.

"You guys meet with the father. Becky and I are going to get some coffee," Bobby said and waited for the nurse to once again gently led him by the elbow toward the cafeteria near the lobby of the hospital.

"Don't be long!" Richard said and smiled wickedly at the couple as they slowly made their way from the crowd.

A few moments later, the distraught father met with Richard, Jim, and Terry.

"I want to thank you, gentlemen, for bringing the gift of life to my daughter. My wife and I will never be able to thank you for what you have done. We tried for so many years to conceive a child and she is our dream come true and we almost lost her. She is our whole world. If we loose her, I don't know what will happen to us...to our marriage."

"It was nothing, really. We are honored to have helped in this small way," Richard said. "Saving lives...well, after seeing so much death...saving lives repays for what we took. What we lost," Richard said, turned and walked away while tears streamed down his face.

The distraught father ran after Richard and asked, "Excuse me, but what did you mean by what you just said?"

"Before you were born, I do believe, I was sent to Vietnam. I took lives, I lost friends, and my damn arm. I never recovered from that and if this is some small gesture of kindness I can return to someone, that is all worth it. I lost a sister and gave away her child. I have wanted to die everyday of my life because I have felt so worthless. This helps," he added.

"My wife is waiting to meet you and your friends" this young man said not knowing what else to say at this time.

"Where is she?" Richard asked.

"She is waiting outside of the operating room. Waiting for news about Sarah."

"Sarah is your baby?"

"Yes. She is only four days old and so weak, but so beautiful. She has her mother's eyes and smile," he added.

"Come on guys. Let's go meet Sarah's mother," Richard said and the foursome left the emergency room waiting area for the third floor.

"By the way, my name is Jason McAllister," Jason said and offered his hand to the three gentlemen while they rode the elevator to the floors above. "I am a state trooper in Arizona and love my job, but now that I have a daughter, I don't know about the risk involved. I want to live long enough to see her grow up, get married and have babies of her own."

"There is risk in any job, Jason," Richard said. "Some people give some and some people give all. Fate is life and life is fate. Nothing we can do or say will change the outcome and I am just coming to realize that, myself. I am finally growing up, I guess. It just took me longer than most people."

Silence enveloped the elevator car while each man thought about what had just been said. Each man thinking about their pasts and futures until the door of the car opened and they exited.

"My wife is over there," Jason said and walked toward his distraught wife.

"Sweetheart, these are the gentlemen who brought Sarah her heart."

"Well, one of our group is downstairs flirting with one of the nurses, but he will join us later, I assume," Richard said and smiled.

"Sweetheart, this is..." Jason began. "I am sorry, but I don't know any of your names," he added.

"My name is Richard Bennett," Richard said and offered his one hand to the slight woman who gently shook his hand in her own.

"This is Terry Connors and my name is Jim Benson. Terry and I were flying the helicopter that crashed and low and behold Richard and his friend, Bobby, happened to be on the spot, in their tractor trailer and they finished the job we started."

"I am very pleased to meet you and my husband and I will never be able to thank you for what you have done," she said timidly.

"Your daughter's name is Sarah, but we don't know your name. I hope you don't mind, but I don't think Mrs. McAllister is what I want to call you," Richard said. "I think we are closer than Mr. Bennett and Mrs. McAllister, don't you?" Richard added trying to ease the tension in the room.

"Yes, please forgive me," Jason said. "This is my lovely wife, Livy and yes, Sarah is our beautiful daughter."

Richard's head snapped around and looked into Livy's eyes while reaching out with his lone hand.

"Your name is Livy?" he asked the woman.

"Why, yes it is, Richard. You looked surprised."

"Your name is Livy?" Richard asked again as if his hearing was impaired along with his arm.

"Livy?" Richard whispered and reached out to touch her face with his hand.

"Are you alright?" Terry asked.

"Livy?" Richard repeated and reached out and hugged the small, frightened woman while shameless tears streamed down his face.

"What in God's name is wrong with you?" Terry continued while Richard wept uncontrollably.

Moments later, Livy eased herself from Richard's arm and helped him sit down while the overwrought man tried to compose himself.

"Do you know my wife?" Jason asked while his mind tried to grasp the meaning of the events that had unfolded since he met Gunnery Sergeant Robert Dragon and now this total stranger who appeared to know his wife.

"I think so," Richard began after Jim Benson handed him a glass of water.

"You said your name is Richard Bennett?" Jason asked.

"Yes, Bennett is my last name."

"You had a sister named Olivia, didn't you?" Jason asked while tears spilled from his eyes.

"Yes, my sister, whom I loved more than life itself, was named Olivia," he said and looked at the mirror image of the sister he lost so many long years ago.

"Olivia was your mother, Livy," Jason began.

"Olivia was my sister," Richard whispered and reached out to accept the hand of his niece he had not seen in thirty years.

"I don't understand," Livy whispered. "All I ever had were letters that had never been mailed to some man named Bobby Dragon and some newspaper clippings about battles in Vietnam, but I threw them out when we began working on the nursery for the baby. I never knew I would have a reason to save them," she added. "I never knew who Olivia Bennett was or Bobby Dragon and to be perfectly honest with you, I really didn't care and don't think I do now," Livy said and stood up. "I have a very sick baby to worry about and that is all I want to worry about now," she said and left the waiting room with her husband on her heels.

"I have to find Bobby," Richard said and ran out of the waiting room to go find his friend.

Just around the corner, Richard met Jason, Livy and close behind was Bobby and his new acquaintance, Becky Smith.

"Bobby!" Richard yelled. "Oh my God! Bobby!" He said a little more quietly after several hospital staff 'shushed' him.

"What in hell is wrong with you, Richard?" Bobby asked.

"I found Livy!" he cried and reached out to touch his frightened niece.

"Livy...this is your father, Bobby Dragon!" Richard exclaimed joyously.

"My father?" Livy whispered while Jason steadied her in his arms.

"Livy?" Bobby said in wide-eyed wonder. "My baby, Livy?" he responded before the shock has worn off.

"I think we need to go into this private office, Becky suggested to the group who slowly made their way from the hallway into a comfortable private lounge.

Bobby reached out and held the hands of his daughter for the first time and stared into the face that, as Richard had noticed, was the mirror image of her mother.

"You are as beautiful as your mother," Bobby said as tears flowed freely from his eyes, as tears also flowed from everyone the eyes of everyone else in the room, now.

"You are so beautiful, Livy," Bobby said and sat down next to this young woman.

"Bobby never knew that he had a daughter or any child, Livy," Richard explained. "Please don't blame him. He never knew. I knew and I take full responsibility for what I did."

"Just what did you do?" Livy asked sternly.

"Your mother died, Livy and you were only a baby and without regard for what Bobby might have thought or did, I sent you to live with foster parents. For that, I will never forgive myself."

"Livy, Richard just told me about all of this, just in the last few days, as a matter of fact. Until just a few days ago, I didn't know any of this myself, but please don't blame Richard. He buried his sister, his mother was hospitalized and he was suffering from his own demons. I have forgiven him and I do hope over time you will, also."

"This is just too confusing for me now. I need to get back to Sarah. We will discuss this at another time. Jason, get their phone numbers and let's go. I have a sick child to take care of," Livy said angrily and left the room.

"Your baby is the baby who needs the new heart, isn't she?" Bobby asked Jason who took out a piece of paper.

"Yes, she is and you men probably saved her life. Livy will realize this in time and she will be as grateful as I am. I can't tell you how grateful I am, Bobby…grateful to all of you for what you have done."

"We were destined to meet, weren't we?" Bobby asked Jason.

"Yes, we were and just after you drove off, I knew you were her father and tried like hell to find you. I had the whole Trooper division looking for you, but you are like a ghost. No I.D., no registered license plate…nothing."

"I know. I do my best work in secret," Bobby said and smiled.

"You aren't going to disappear, now, are you?" Jason asked.

"Not on your life, Mister! I just found my daughter and now I have a granddaughter who needs me. I am not going anywhere!"

"Thank God!" Maybe now we can find some peace. Livy has always had this empty hole in her soul. She never knew about her family and now, maybe you can bring her some peace."

"Well, the story she will learn in not pleasant and she may be disappointed in the truth."

"The truth is all she wants," Jason said.

"When she is ready, I will tell her everything she wants to know and Richard can fill her in on what I don't know."

"I will tell her all I know about Gunnery Sergeant Robert Dragon," Jason said with pride.

"I will tell her all about her father, if you don't mind." Bobby said. "Sometimes fact and fiction get mixed up and I want her to know the truth about my life," he said quietly.

"I respect that. I am sorry," Jason said. "I am just so proud of you and now…imagine that…you are my father-in-law! Wow!"

"I am a humble man and don't talk about the past very much. I will talk about it one time and one time only."

"We will both appreciate this and accept that. Now, I really have to go see how Sarah is doing."

"We will wait with you," Bobby said and the whole room emptied out and went to the operating waiting room on the next floor.

Several silent hours past, without any words spoken, but Bobby noticed Livy kept looking at him, when she didn't think he was watching. Bobby's training came in handy. He had his own daughter under surveillance without her being aware. He was enjoying seeing her face…the same likeness of the woman he would always love in his heart.

Becky and her friend, another nurse, Ivy Patten brought in coffee, soda and sandwiches for the group to eat while they waited for news on Sarah's condition.

"Richard, Bobby and others, I want you to meet my best friend, Ivy Patten. She and I are house-mates and we wondered if you would all like to come to our house for dinner."

"What time?" Richard said after he jumped to his feet, reaching out to shake Ivy's hand.

"Don't be shy, Richard," Bobby teased.

"I really am shy," Richard said while he pumped Ivy's hand in an enthusiastic greeting.

"I can see that," Ivy said while flirting with Bobby's friend.

"We will see you all at the house at seven o'clock this evening if you like. Bobby knows the address," Becky said. "We both have to get back to work now, so please feel free to stop over later," she said as both women left the room.

"I think we will have to pass," Terry said with Jim in agreement. "We have to get home."

"We will call you and let you know how Sarah is doing and once again, thank you for saving my granddaughter's life," Bobby said. "I love the sound of that. My granddaughter" he repeated.

"We will take a rain check, also," Jason said. "My family will be back shortly and we are going to sit here until we can take Sarah home. My folks and other relatives went home for a few hours to get some clean clothes and things."

"You have a large family?" Bobby asked.

"Yes, they are wonderful and they love Livy to pieces."

"I am glad she has them and has apparently fallen in love with a wonderful man, as well," Bobby said.

"I am very thankful for what I have," Livy said. "I will also be thankful for what I will have," she said and smiled for the first time at her father.

Bobby slowly stood up and walked over to his daughter, reached out and without any hesitation, Livy stood up, grasped his outstretched hand and fell into her father's warm embrace where they stood, crying like babies, for many long moments.

"I am so sorry. I never knew," Bobby whispered into her ear. "I never had any idea."

Livy released herself from his embrace and looked him in his tear stained eyes.

"My mother. Tell me about my mother," she whispered. "What happened to her?"

Bobby took her small hand in his and led his daughter from the room and outside on a picnic bench where he told her all about her mother. How they met, how they fell in love and the life he hoped they would have had. He told her that she indeed took her own life, but it wasn't her fault and he insisted she never blame her mother for what she had done. He assured her he had and always would love her mother and her and her family.

Bobby also told her that Richard had been a homeless veteran who had spent every day, for over, thirty years, to find her. He confirmed that Richard had sacrificed his own happiness and any life he could have had to right the wrong he had committed.

Bobby also told her how he and Richard had just met…fate he called it…at just this time and that fate again, had intervened to unite them in the quest to save Sarah's life.

Richard came running outside to get Bobby and Livy.

"The doctors want to see you!" Richard cried with excitement. "Everything went well!" he added.

The group, including Jason's family, was gathered for a conference with the surgeons who performed the surgery and they indeed were hopeful that Sarah would recover, fully, in time.

Tears of happiness, joy and peace filled the room along with hugs and kisses from all.

Jason's father walked up to Bobby and Richard and thanked them for filling a void in Livy's life after explaining all that Jason had done to track him down since he met him on the highway days before.

"She always felt empty, inside. There were so many questions about her past they she needed answers for and now, she may…she will have some peace. For that, I will never be able to thank you," Mr. McAllister said.

"I want to thank you for raising such a fine son and welcoming my daughter into your lives like your own. She was lucky to have you," Bobby confirmed.

"Can I see Sarah?" Bobby asked Livy.

"She is in ICU, but we can look in the window," she offered and took her father's elbow and they left the room to see their precious little girl.

Tears filled his once brave Marine's eyes, again while he prayed for the good health of his granddaughter and her family for over an hour.

Jason, Livy and his family stayed at the hospital and Bobby and Richard told them they were leaving for a short time for dinner with Becky and Ivy, but assured them they would be back later that evening.

Six Months Later

Bobby and Richard traversed the countryside in the roaming Vietnam Wall on wheels picking up the government supplies in Boston and making timely deliveries at Camp Pendleton, but now, their route included extra stops along the way. Each time the duo passed through Arizona, they stopped to see Livy and her family and Becky and Ivy.

On this one particular evening, Bobby and Becky were babysitting for Sarah while Livy and Jason went out for an evening of romance that included dining and dancing.

Becky was rocking Sarah in his arms, smiling down at the tiny baby who was gaining strength by the day. As all baby's do, Sarah began to wail for no apparent reason and wouldn't calm down.

"I don't know what's wrong with her Bobby," Becky said. "I just changed her diaper and she has been fed."

"Well, she probably misses her old grandfather," Bobby said and removed the fussing child from Becky's arms.

Bobby sat down in another rocking chair and began to talk to the now screaming child.

"Now, now, hush...be still my heart," he began. "You don't want to get yourself all worked up now. You are a little trooper and you don't want to get yourself all upset for nothing, do you?"

Sarah immediately stopped crying at the comforting words she heard spoken from her grandfather. Her eyes remained steadfastly gazed into the blue eyes of her own flesh and blood.

"Do you want to know about your grandmother, Sarah?" he asked the infant, totally unaware that Becky was still in the room.

"Your grandmother was the most beautiful woman in the world, Sarah. She looks just like your mother and you. No, she didn't have your bright red hair, but that is your father's contribution to your beauty, my dear. Your grandmother was so sweet, soft and tender. She didn't have a mean bone in her body," Bobby continued to ramble as he slowly rocked in the chair with her granddaughter. "I have missed your grandmother every day since I last saw her and I always will."

Becky stood up and began to leave the room, as tears cascaded down her cheeks.

Bobby finally realized she was still in the room and hadn't meant to speak out loud about his feeling for the woman who had been dead for so many years, now.

"Wait, Becky. Please don't go. I am not finished yet," Bobby pleaded.

Somberly, Becky remained standing in the doorway, but her tears had not stopped.

"Becky, I was just telling Sarah about her grandmother and my feelings for her, but I also wanted to tell her about my feelings for you, if you will let me," Bobby whispered as Sarah's eyes closed and her breathing softened.

"What are your feelings for me?" Becky asked remaining at the doorway.

"My love for Olivia has grown over the years, I guess, because I haven't fallen in love with anyone else. I guess I have built a fantasy out of what might have been to keep my sanity. I have made her an idol and worshiped her, but having met you, I realize it's time to let her rest in peace and in doing so, I realize I have fallen in love with you and you, my love, are the most beautiful woman in the world and if you..."

"Bobby, you are still in love with Olivia..."

"Please let me finish, Becky."

"I love Olivia because she is my guardian angel now. She, I feel, is responsible for all the events that have taken place over the last six months. I truly believe she arranged this whole situation from Heaven. I believe she orchestrated my whole life since I lost her. She allowed me to suffer the pain of her loss, the loss of my best friend, to make me a better man. I believe she knew I had suffered enough and it was time for me to have a life of my own filled with love and happiness and since I have met Livy, Sarah, Jason, and yes, even Richard, and especially having met you, my love, my life is more complete than I could have ever hoped for."

Becky came and stood in front of the rocking chair that seated Sarah and her grandfather and gently took the sleeping infant from his arms and carefully laid her in her brass cradle.

Bobby stood from the chair and asked Becky to sit on the couch. On one knee, Bobby removed a royal blue velvet covered box from his pants pocket and opened it. Inside was the most beautiful emerald ring Becky had ever seen. It was oval in shape and surrounded in tiny sparking diamonds.

"Becky, no one has filled my heart and soul with more joy and happiness than you have and if you would have me as your husband, I would be honored to have you as my wife. Please marry me, sweetheart. I love you with my whole heart and soul."

"I have loved you since the first moment I saw you, Bobby. No man has ever shown so much compassion for any human beings as you have. You risked life and limb for those you served with in Vietnam and you continued to help those in need…those you didn't realize you already knew as time has gone on. I have watched your face as you hold your granddaughter and speak with your daughter. You are an amazing man and there is no man I would want to marry, other than you, Bobby, but only…but only if you feel Olivia would approve."

"I know she has given me her blessing, Beck. I know in my heart she has set me free!"

"Please tell me you will be my wife."

"I will marry you, Bobby and I will be everything you want in a wife."

"You already are, Becky…you already are," he said and he swept her off her feet and carried her into her bedroom for the remainder of the evening.

Theirs was not the only good news to be had on that one night. Richard and Ivy had become engaged at that same time and Livy told Jason they were expecting another baby in eight more months.

The Wedding

Bobby and Richard were best men at each of their weddings, which just so happened to be on the same day, at the same church.

Bobby had no family to attend, with the exception of his daughter and granddaughter. Richard, unfortunately, had no relatives in attendance with the exception of his niece and her daughter, but Jason's family and Becky's and Ivy's families more than made up for the loss of any real close kin. Bobby and Richard now were members of a large, close-knit, and happy family; of which no one could ask for more.

The blissfully happy couples decided to travel together to honeymoon in Hawaii for a month of fun in the sun, but unbeknownst to anyone else, Bobby had an announcement to make. The newlyweds and the family members were gathered at the reception that was held in a lovely old Arizona church and ready to say their farewells as Bobby began to speak.

"I realize what I am about to say is probably not...well, shall I say, not timed very well, but I have something I have to do before I embark on my new life with my wife and new family," Bobby said while the crowd held their breath for what appeared to be very bad news.

Bobby looked deeply into Becky's eyes and saw the horror that filled them, the questions that obviously filled her mind, along with everyone else's.

"Becky, I wanted to marry you before I told you what the plan is for the next few years of my life will be. I was afraid to tell you before because I was afraid of what you would say."

"Bobby...this is not the time for any rash statements!" Richard barked.

"Oh, I also forgot to tell you, Richard because this involves you and your wife as well," he said without expression.

"What in God's name are you blabbering about?" Richard asked angrily.

"Have you ever been to the Vietnam Wall in Washington?" Bobby asked all those in attendance.

"No," everyone responded.

"Well, I never had the courage to face that wall myself and by God, I am going to do that before we go to Hawaii! That is where my next journey will begin, my friends and family."

"We would love to visit the Wall, Bobby. What makes you think we wouldn't want to go there with you?" Becky asked and hugged Bobby tightly.

"I said, that is just the beginning of our future...at the Wall. From there, we will go on our honeymoon to Hawaii, as planned, but then, we are going to Vietnam!"

"You want to go back to visit Vietnam?" Richard asked as if Bobby had grown another head in the last minute or two.

"I am not going back to visit Vietnam. I am going back to bring Johnny home!"

"I am not leaving Vietnam without knowing what happened to my best friend, Johnny. If it takes two months or ten years, I am not leaving that country without something of my friend. I left him there and it has torn my heart out of my body all these years." If no one wants to go, fine...I am going with or without you!" he yelled and ran from the reception hall.

Becky ran outside and stood before the man who cried shameless tears. She reached out and he fell into her waiting arms while they both cried tears for each other.

"I will follow you to the ends of the earth, Bobby. You already knew that, didn't you?" Becky asked and smiled amid her tears.

"Yes, I already knew that!" he said and smiled as well.

Richard and Ivy met the couple, while the others remained inside the church vestibule to give them some privacy.

"I owe you my life, Bobby. Ivy and I will accompany you to Vietnam and we will find Johnny!" he said and embraced the other newlywed couple.

"I have arranged everything, down to the last detail. He have scouts who will help us, housing has all been arranged and all the comforts of home will be there when we arrive. I also have some information that I haven't ever told anyone...never admitted it to myself, but I truly believe he is still alive! I know he was seeing a beautiful Vietnamese girl and I almost think that whole event was set up. I find it odd that I was allowed to live. I think he loved that woman and just wanted to be with her. Knowing how much I loved Olivia and now love Becky, I can understand. I couldn't imagine it then, but now I understand. I just want to find him and know he is safe!"

"You think he is still alive?" Richard asked in amazement.

"I do and if he is, I want him to come home, if he wants to."

"Do you think he would want to, after all this time?"

"Yes., I do. I imagine he has always wanted to, but was afraid of imprisonment or more afraid of me finding him!"

"Wouldn't he face charges?" Richard asked.

"I have already gotten that taken care of. He will have an new identity. I persuaded some very influential people that he had been working under-cover all these years!"

"Oh, no one in their right mind would buy that." Richard scoffed.

"No one said that person is in their right mind," Bobby said and laughed.

"Who is it?" Richard asked with the others as curious as well.

"Only the president and I would know who it is!" Bobby said mysteriously and snickered.

WASHINGTON, D.C.
2003

"Colonel Blackburn, there is a call for you. It's President Ward."

"Thank you Jennifer. I will take the call in my office," John Blackburn said and retreated to his office.

Before John spoke to President Ward he walked to the large window, in his simple office, that faced the White House. Taking a deep breath he picked up the receiver and greeted the President; the commander in chief of the United States.

"Good afternoon, President Ward. What can I do for you?"

"John, I received a call from Bobby and he has plans to go to Vietnam to find you and bring you home. He asked me to make whatever arrangements I could manage for him and the people who would accompany him."

"Do you know when he plans to leave?"

"He told me he wanted to leave immediately, but I convinced him to meet me here first," the President assured his friend. "I told him I wanted to discuss some things with him at a private dinner, tomorrow night."

"Is he going to come?" John asked.

"Yes, he said he would be honored. He also said he would accept my offer to have his group be transported to Washington by my private jet. They will arrive tomorrow afternoon at 2:00. He did mention he wanted to visit the Vietnam Wall as soon as his entourage arrived."

"I will wait for him there, Bill. I know what panel he will visit, first," John Blackburn sadly confirmed. "Thank you."

"This is not going to be easy for either of you, you know, John."

"I know, Bill, but it is time. I can't have him going over there chasing a ghost," John said honestly.

"You will come to the dinner, also, tomorrow night, won't you?"

"If Bobby wants me there, I will be there."

"Okay, John. See you tomorrow night," the President said and disconnected the call.

"Yeah, maybe," John whispered into the line that was already dead.

"You must really be someone special to have President Ward offer to have us come to Washington and use his private jet," Richard said with Ivy, Becky and even Bobby in total agreement as the foursome departed the jet and headed in a rental car toward the Vietnam Wall.

"President Ward and I go way back," Bobby confirmed. "He was my commanding officer in Nam. He and I were the last two people to see Johnny alive. He owes me. It was because of him I was dragged back to base camp without finding my best friend," Bobby said gritting his teeth.

"I'm sure he had his reasons," Richard said. "He probably knew Johnny couldn't or wouldn't be found alive and didn't want you to die, too."

"Yeah, well, whatever his reasons were, I never agreed with them and never will," Bobby said as he and his wife and friends parked the car and began walking toward the black granite wall that held the names of more than fifty eight thousand young men and women who had given their lives for a war no one understood.

"I would like a few minutes alone, if you all don't mind," Bobby said and without waiting for a response left those who accompanied him and began to walk to the panel that held Johnny Blackburn's name.

Bobby approached the panel while tears welled up in his eyes. His hands shook as he reached up to caress the name of his childhood friend and comrade in arms without noticing the lone figure who approached him from behind.

"Bobby," a voice whispered from a few feet behind the former Marine sniper.

Bobby turned around and looked into the eyes of a man who had tears in his own eyes.

"Johnny?" Bobby whispered in disbelief.

"Yes, Bobby; it's me."

For the first time in his life, Bobby Dragon was speechless and stood totally still in shock.

Bobby looked at the man who had been his best friend in times of joy and times of sadness, turned and began to walk away.

"Bobby! Wait!" Johnny yelled after his friend.

"You come near me, you fucking bastard and I will kill you!" Bobby swore with the veins on his forehead nearly erupting from the anger he was trying to control.

"Bobby, please wait!" Johnny yelled while breaking into a run to catch his former friend.

Bobby stopped running and turned around to face the man who had caught up to him.

"I just told you, if you come near me your mother fucker, I will kill you with my bare hands!"

"You have to let me explain!" Johnny yelled after the man who now quickly walked to meet his wife and friends who looked on in horror.

"What in hell is going on?" Richard asked while he stood in between this man and his friend.

"Friends, let me introduce you to a man whom I thought was missing all these damn years! This, my wife and friends is the mysterious Johnny Blackburn who tore my heart out the day the VC dragged his ass away or was it the VC, Johnny? Let me answer that question, for you, you fucking bastard. I guess they weren't VC, were they?"

"Bobby, you have to let me explain!"

"You have had over thirty years to do any explaining you might have had to do, you bastard!" Bobby screamed in a rage while he grabbed this man by the neck with his hands.

"I will kill you where you stand, you mother fucker!" Bobby said while Richard tried to pry his hands loose with his one arm.

"Bobby, please!" Becky screamed while the security staff that surrounds the Vietnam Wall ran to intervene; to break up the ruckus that had broken out on this sacred ground.

"Okay, break it up, you two," one police officer said while two other officers pried Bobby's hands from around Johnny's neck.

From the shadows another figure, dressed in black from head to foot and wearing sunglasses approached the assembled group.

"Bobby…John, come with me," the solitary figure demanded with explicit and unquestionable authority. "Will you other folks please excuse us for a few moments," the mysterious figure said and without waiting for a response, herded the two men toward a waiting vehicle, an impressive Suburban that displayed official government license plates.

"Holy shit, what in hell is going on?" Richard asked while the two women looked on in a state of shock of their own.

"I have no idea!" Becky responded while their group sat on nearby granite benches to wait for Bobby and the other man to reappear.

"That has to be Johnny Blackburn," Richard commented before this trio continued to sit and wonder what was going on inside the large government vehicle that was parked nearby.

"Bobby, John said he wanted to meet with you, here, alone, but I assumed the shock of this development would escalate into some sort of confrontation, so I made it a point to greet you here, myself, as well. I hope you don't mind the intrusion," President Ward said after removing his sunglasses.

"Bill, I have no idea what in hell is going on here and what has been going on for over thirty years, but to be honest with you, I really don't give a flying fuck!" Bobby said and tried to exit the vehicle.

"Listen to what I have to say, Bobby and then you can choose to do what you feel is best," Bill said with the authority he demanded of his soldiers so long ago.

"Make it quick," Bobby said while glaring at both men who sat opposite him in the rear of the government vehicle.

"First of all, John had nothing to do with his own disappearance in Vietnam," the United States President began. "I wanted both of you to be involved in the final segment of the super secret missions we were undertaking, but after what you had been through, with the loss of the woman you loved, I knew you were distracted and you know as well as I do, that can be deadly for you and the men who served under you. Even you have to admit you were not in top form after the death of Olivia," Bill said with Bobby nodding his head, sadly, in agreement.

"You will never know what a painful decision that was for me to separate you two men at that point and to continue with a charade all these years. I have gone over that decision nearly everyday since...wondering if I did the right thing and even though I will never know the pain I have inflicted on you, thinking your best friend was captured, tortured or worse, I still agree with that decision I made. If I had not done what I did, I feel one or both of you would honestly have your name engraved on that wall with all the other heroes of that era."

"Okay, you have apologized enough, Bill and I have heard how sorry you are. Now, explain what in hell it was all about!" Bobby demanded while continuing to glare at both men.

"That's fair," Bill said before continuing with his story. "As you know, you were sent state-side right after Johnny's apparent abduction. I realized you had suffered enough, but I still needed one or two men I could trust beyond a shadow of a doubt to finish what had already begun. The negotiations to release all the remaining POW's in Vietnam. The negotiations, as you know, had broken down and we were at a stalemate. Johnny offered himself as 'bait', so to speak, to appear to be captured and with trusted South Vietnamese citizens, dressed as VC, approached the largest POW camp in Hanoi with their "captive" and once the gates were open, our meager group overtook the guards and within seconds, helicopters landed in the middle of the camp and all POW's were securely and safely evacuated."

"Well, that is very nice and I am pleased that your mission was successful, but why the secrecy and why in hell did you let me believe you were dead all these years, you fucker?" Bobby spat at his former friend.

"That was my idea as well," the President responded before Johnny could speak.

"Oh? Was it because you thought I couldn't handle the pressure of discovering you didn't trust me? Was it because you thought it was better that I suffer every fucking day of my life…missing my friend? Well, which was it?" Bobby demanded.

"I have been working for the government all these years," John began before the President could start to explain.

"Well, so have I," Bobby began. "I have been delivering stupid weapons in a tractor trailer all these years back and forth across the God damn country. Isn't that an honor? Wow! I bet you are impressed, aren't you Johnny? What have you been doing for the government? Bring secrets from Asia to the United States in secure brief cases…attached to your wrist with a chain bracelet? I bet you are a God dam Major, aren't you?" Bobby yelled without taking a breath in between accusations.

"John is a Colonel," Bill said while Bobby's raised his eyebrows in disbelief.

"Well, I guess I don't deserve to be in the company of such influential people, now do I?" Bobby said and opened the door to the vehicle and departed.

"Get your ass back in this vehicle, soldier and let me finish!" Bill demanded.

Bobby sat back down in his seat, folded his arms and glared at both men, silently.

"You have both been working, with honor, for the government all these years, Bobby. You have not been just delivering stupid weapons, as you call them, across the United States in a tractor trailer. I can't even tell you what you have been delivering all these years and even John doesn't know what he has been doing, in all truthfulness. He trusts me to do what is right and completes his missions without question, as you have, but you just didn't know it."

"There are no two men in this whole country that I trust more than you and John, Bobby. I always have and always will."

"I am a meager Gunny Sgt. and Johnny is a Colonel?" Bobby asked with obvious hurt in his expression.

"You two were always so competitive," the President said and laughed. "No, Bobby, if you had bothered to look at your papers the government sends you now and then, you would notice your pay increases are the equivalent of a colonel, yourself, but you never did bother with paperwork, did you?" the man continued and chuckled.

"No, I never did bother with that shit. I can't be bothered with the trivial," he admitted.

"You don't even know how much money you have, do you?" Johnny asked and smiled.

"No, I have no idea and don't care. Money means nothing to me. I have been consumed with thinking about those I loved and lost and that includes you, you bastard!" Bobby said, reached out and grasped his friends hands in his own.

"Have there been times when you thought you had seen me, Bobby? Times when you felt me close to you?" John asked and smiled.

"Yeah, as a matter of fact I have mentioned to Richard, several times, that I swore to God I had seen you pull up for fuel while we were fueling up or I swore I had caught a glimpse of you driving by on the highway or passing by in a damn grocery store, Johnny."

"Well, Bobby, it wasn't your imagination! I have been keeping an eye on you now and then to make sure you are okay. Do you remember the tractor trailer that drove by you, not so long ago and blasted the air horn while you were laying on the ground? Well, my friend that was me!" Johnny said and laughed.

"I was even in the hospital when you brought that heart in for your granddaughter."

"You always were like shit, Johnny. Always around when you weren't useful," Bobby said and smiled.

"It is time to move on, now Bobby. It is time to forget the past and live in the present and think of the future," John said and smiled.

"I have already begun, John. I just married the most wonderful woman in the world and now can begin a new life from this day forward with a new friend I have just met. What did you say your name is Colonel?"

"My name is Colonel John Blackburn and your name is?"

"His name is Colonel Robert Dragon," President Bill Ward said.

"Nice to meet you," Bobby said and hugged his new friend while both men cried tears of joy and sadness at the same time.

"Please come with me," Bobby said to both men. "I have some very special people I want you to meet," he said while John and Bill accompanied the newlywed to meet his friends and wife.

Bobby never forgot the first love of his life; his Olivia. He felt she was guiding him every day in the direction he needed to be led in, at the appropriate time in his life.

Contrary to those memories, neither Colonel John Blackburn or Colonel Robert Dragon ever mentioned the past again. The present and future with their new found families and friends were all either men were concerned about. Their friendship and loyalties continued from that day forward, from where it left off over thirty years before.

THE END